Heath Taws is a simple man. Born and raised in Panama City, Florida, he finds himself 24 years old and engaged to the love of his life. Heath enjoys reading comic books, collecting odd curios, and making movies with friends. He is currently finishing his bachelor's degree in Biblical and Theological Studies at Covenant College. He considers himself abundantly blessed, and is very thankful for his family and future wife. This is his first book. "He must become greater; I must become less." John 3:30

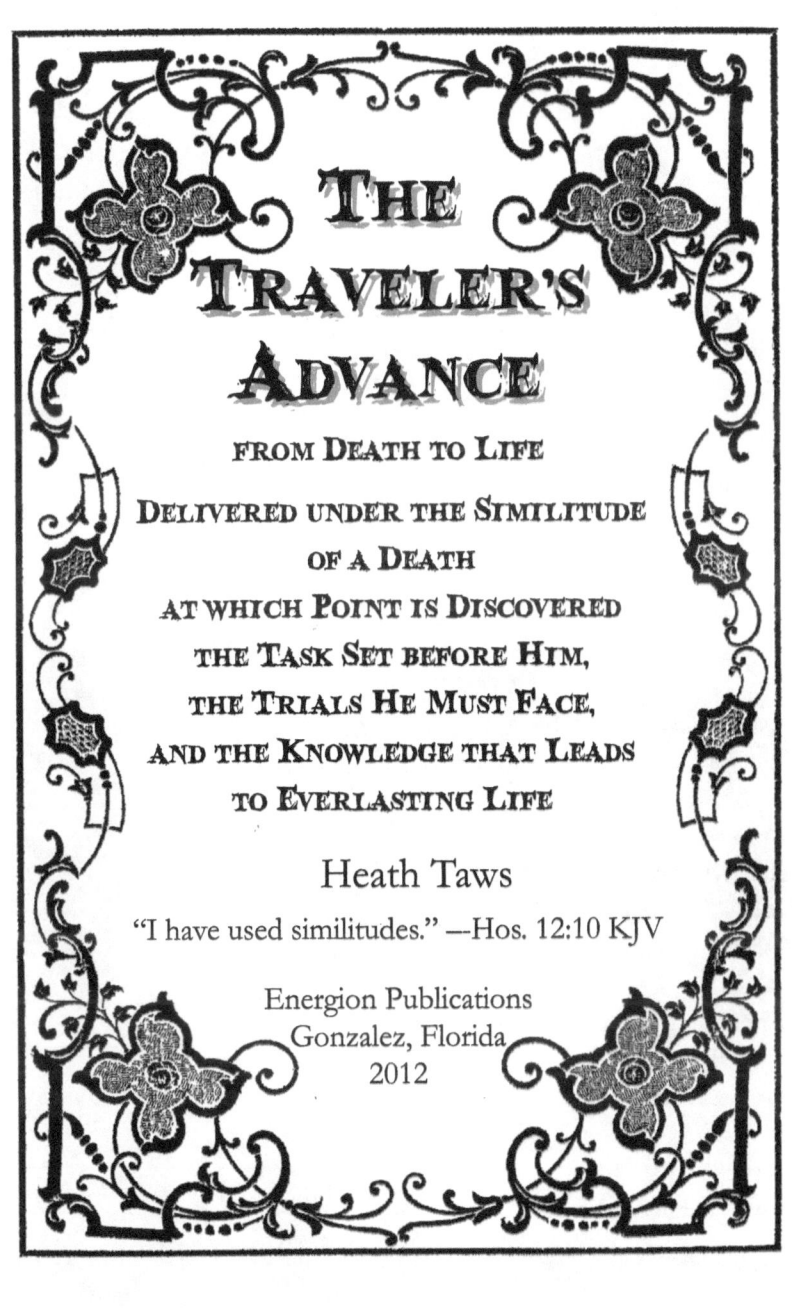

THE TRAVELER'S ADVANCE

FROM DEATH TO LIFE

DELIVERED UNDER THE SIMILITUDE
OF A DEATH
AT WHICH POINT IS DISCOVERED
THE TASK SET BEFORE HIM,
THE TRIALS HE MUST FACE,
AND THE KNOWLEDGE THAT LEADS
TO EVERLASTING LIFE

Heath Taws

"I have used similitudes." —Hos. 12:10 KJV

Energion Publications
Gonzalez, Florida
2012

Cover Design: Nick May
Illustrations: Chris Blake

ISBN10: 1-938434-03-X
ISBN13: 978-1-938434-03-7
Library of Congress Control Number: 2012938017

Energion Publications
P. O. Box 841
Gonzalez, FL 32560

850-525-3916
www.energionpubs.com

This Book is dedicated to my nephew Connor.
May you always walk the narrow path ...

TABLE OF CONTENTS

EMBARK

STUMBLE

TRIUMPH

Author's Apology

"As I walked through the wilderness of this world ..."

The word apology can mean two different things. The first is the most commonly known and it means to ask for forgiveness or show regret or remorse. The second and more uncommon definition is that an apology is a defense, excuse, or justification for something. This story is my apology.

Before I move on, let me just say that if you have read this far then you have already read more of the introduction than I ever do ... so ... thanks. This story came pretty naturally to me because it is my story. Better yet, it is your story. It is the story of a guy who thought he had it all figured out, but in reality, had it all wrong.

This story is my apology to God for my rebellious nature, my confession that I will never go back to living as a slave, and finally, it is my argument against sin and all the wiles of the Devil. It is a fictional account of a path that we all must take. A path that has massive eternal ramifications for all of our lives.

I hope that as you read this story the deeper meanings will not be lost on you. I hope that you will replace the main characters name with your own at times, and bask in the depravity and the beauty of the message before you. The concepts and themes of this book run through our hearts, and I hope this message will be relatable to you, the reader, just as it is to me.

Thanks for reading, and I hope you enjoy, The Traveler's Advance!

PART ONE:

EMBARK

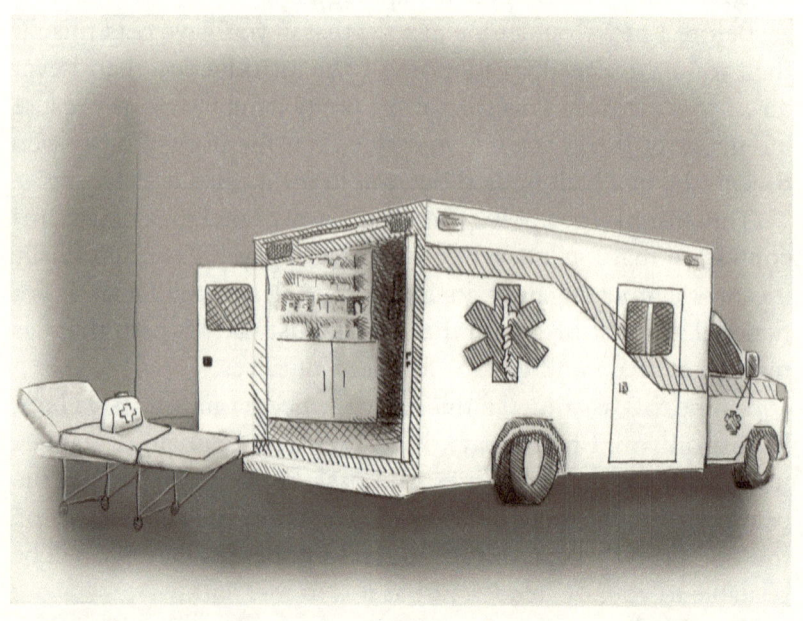

1

SINISTER BIZARRERIE

J•OSHUA AWOKE IN DARKNESS, searching his body for the bullet holes which he knew should be there; but weren't. He found no wounds, nor did he feel any pain, except for the back of his head. But, come to think of it, he couldn't quite remember why he was checking for wounds in the first place or why his head hurt for that matter. He still had on his white dress shirt that he was wearing when he left the house that morning. Only this time it was covered in blood and badly torn. He also still had on his favorite pair of jeans which were now shredded in such a way that Joshua would have probably paid more for them had they started out like this in the store.

"How did I get here?" Joshua asked himself. "Must … remember," he thought, as he rubbed the back of his head which stung for no apparent reason.

The last thing he could recall was walking down a well-lit street towards his favorite dive to meet his buddy A-Chan for a drink. But now, he was surrounded by darkness. That is, of course, with the exception of a beam of light that was coming from a door which stood ajar about twenty feet in front of him. Everything was the same except for, well, everything. He also noticed that he now had shackles around his wrists and ankles; shackles that had always been there, but, until now, were invisible to him. They didn't really impair his movement at all, but they were heavy and annoying. Each shackle had what felt to Joshua, in the dark, like multiple chain loops. The weight of the chains had to be around one pound each with seven loops attached to either side. He could feel markings on the sides, but in the dark, he couldn't make out their inscription.

"Kidnapped!" Joshua thought to himself. "I must have been kidnapped! I am chained up in some cell by some radical terrorist group probably hoping to squeeze a few pennies out of my dad! Well, good luck to them. I doubt dad will even care."

Ideas of how this whole thing must have occurred ran through his head.

"I must have been drugged at the bar, or maybe it was A-Chan who planned it. I always knew he was jealous of me!"

Joshua staggered to his feet with all these thoughts in mind, as an ominous, shrouded figure that had been kneeling in the corner stepped into the light from the doorway. A chill ran down Joshua's spine, and his skin broke out with goose-flesh. What was it his mom used to say when he would get a chill? "Someone must be walking on your grave, Joshua!" All of mom's little sayings had an ironic way of creeping up at strange times. The shrouded man smelt like everything awful in the world (assuming this creature even was a man). No, this was not a man. This was something different; something inhuman.

"Get up," the shrouded figure said in a haunting voice.

"Who are you?" Joshua asked. "Where am I? Why have you kidnapped me? You won't get any money from my dad if that's what you're hoping! Ahhhh!" Joshua was once again struck with pain from the back of his head, and he rubbed it hoping that it would just go away.

"Please … what have you done to me? Just let me go, please. I think I need a hospital."

But Joshua knew this monster was not going to give him medical attention. He had only asked out of hope. The cell he was in smelt like a sewer, and somehow, he knew this creature was either the rat king himself or one of his minions. Terrorists never did care much for personal hygiene or cleanliness, and that was never more apparent than when the shrouded man approached Joshua who was crouched on the floor. The cloaked figure knelt down and breathed deeply into Joshua's face, letting out a sickening laugh.

"You are not kidnapped, Joshua—at least not in the full sense of the word," the shrouded figure said. "Do you not recognize this place you're in? Why my boy, this is your home! You have always lived here; your body has just been away on vacation!" A hideous coughing laugh could be heard from underneath the hood that covered the man's face.

"I don't understand," Joshua protested. "What do you mean my home? And my body? On vacation? What organization are you with? Just give me a phone and I will make a call. All of this can be over very soon once I get your money." Joshua's voice was becoming fast and frantic, and his heart began to race inside his chest.

"Money?" the creature asked. "Why should I need money, when Mammon is a close friend of mine? And as I said before, you have not been kidnapped, Joshua, you are dead."

"Dead," Joshua thought, "I can't be dead." But somehow he knew he was. Somehow he had known it all along.

"If I am dead, Mr. Terrorist, then what is this supposed to be? Hell?" Joshua said with a quiet scoff.

"Hell! You think this is Hell!?" The cloaked figure said mockingly. "If you think this is Hell, then you are in for a real treat once we actually get there! Obviously you are having some trouble remembering exactly how you got here, am I right?"

"Yes," Joshua replied, "but I am sure that's just the side effects from whatever drug you gave me."

"Joshua," the cloaked man said, "listen carefully to what I am saying because I will not repeat myself anymore. You are currently gone from your physical body. You are dead. I gave you no drugs, nor did I kidnap you. I am simply here to transport you from one location to another. That is all. I am afraid I have urgent business elsewhere at the moment, which works in your favor. Not long from now your memory will return, and shortly thereafter, I shall return to collect you. And don't worry about the being dead thing. Aren't all humans dead from birth?"

Joshua wasn't sure what he meant by this, but he kept listening—trying to get a grasp on his current situation. His fight or flight mechanism had also begun to kick in and the thought of rushing the man and forcing himself through the door crept into his mind.

"You *could* try to escape like you are thinking, Joshua, but I would just overpower you." Joshua was stunned at the shrouded man's words.

He continued, "Now, where was I? Oh yes, the matter of your soul! It is very much intact; but I'm afraid it must remain here until I can properly escort you to your most deserved and ... undesired destination. It used to be an instant trip, you see, but since my master has gone missing, things have become, how do you say ... complicated?" From underneath the hood came that same coughing, wheezing laugh, and Joshua's hopes of escape left with the silence that followed it.

"Your master?" Joshua asked. "But I don't understand who ..."

"Of course you don't understand," the monster sneered. "You don't understand because you are a fool. You lived like a fool, and you died like a fool. And now, you ignorant boy, you shall live like a cinder. Your name shall be agony and your days shall be...unpleasant, to say the least. But how rude of me!"

Trembling, Joshua watched on as he saw the shrouded man bow before him. He could hear the sound of bones popping, like a pitcher working his knuckles before a big game.

"My name is Skinless ... at least, that is what I have come to be called. My name is of little importance to you, though. My Master's name, however, is of great import'. I serve the great and powerful Death, and well, as I mentioned before, he's gone missing. That is why you will stay here in this cell until my master returns. Like I said, things were so much simpler just a few days ago, but I can't stay here reminiscing about the good ole' days with the likes of you. I have much work to do. I shall return when ... my master returns. Then I will escort you, personally, to the Abyss—or as you humans call it—Hell."

Joshua stared up into the darkness of Skinless' face, and felt his insides churn. Why couldn't he remember how he got here, and was he really dead after all? Would he be escorted to see a man in a red suit with a pitchfork like all the old paintings and cartoons depicted? He was starting to think this scenario more and more unlikely by the second.

Skinless laughed as he stared at Joshua. He turned, opened the cell door, and as he left he muttered something under his breath. Joshua could barely make out what Skinless said (or perhaps he heard perfectly and didn't want to admit it).

"An eternity of pain for a life without shame.
Wait for the fire, your sins fan the flames."

The door slammed shut.

2
A Cruel, Dark World

J·OSHUA STRUGGLED TO REMEMBER the events that led up to his imprisonment. It had all happened so fast at the time, and trying to remember now was like looking at a developing Polaroid picture. It was dark at first, but slowly an image was materializing. The memories were trickling back into his mind like a leaky faucet, and then all at once, it was as if the faucet broke, and the memories came flooding back into his brain.

He remembered falling backwards in an alleyway in great pain. He thought of his life as it flashed before his eyes. Images of his friends and family zoomed past. He thought of his mistakes and of how much the pavement stung beneath his head. He thought of his job. Of all the beautiful women he would never kiss again. Words of hope he had once heard bounced around inside his head. He thought of his bank account and how much money was still inside, or why he ever cared. Those words of hope that flitted through his brain like butterflies had suddenly begun to vanish, and instead, were being replaced with all of his mistakes in life. He thought of the bullets inside his body, of what a cruel world he lived in, and how he had taken part in it; and loved it …

In remembering all these things, he wondered why he had chosen to take *that* particular road at *that* particular time of night, and why he had decided to investigate the scream he heard in the alleyway. He had seen people being mugged before but always acted with means of self-preservation; after all, it was probably just some kids messing with a homeless guy … harmless. As he turned the corner into the alleyway, however, he was confronted with the realization that it was not some smelly old hobo being mugged, but a young woman. His mind said run, everything inside him said run, but he couldn't. His eyes locked with the mugger's, and in those eyes, he saw himself. He saw a desperate man just trying to make his way in the world. He couldn't have even been much older than Joshua by the looks of him.

The mugger released the girl, who, in turn, quickly ran past Joshua, brushing his shoulder with hers as she fled. Did she whisper a thank you as she ran past, or was it just the wind? He wasn't sure, but he didn't care. What he was doing now was beyond a thank you. What he was doing now, was being a hero. The stuff of storybooks, movies, and…local news channels. He was staring down an armed man with nothing more than his class ring and his designer shoes for an arsenal. Just like in the movies, he would charge headfirst into this man and save the day.

Unfortunately, this was not the movies. The mugger turned, noticing Joshua standing in the middle of the alleyway. With shakiness in his voice, he screamed out for Joshua to keep on his way, but he stood his ground. The man held the gun in his quivering, sweaty hand, and screamed once more. Joshua felt the ground shift beneath his feet, and noticed that the world was now moving in slow motion around him. He saw the graffitied concrete walls on either side begin to race past him, like an artist's telling a story of hope, trying to redeem this dark alley. He was running, slow at first, but gaining speed. His eyes still locked with the mugger's. The man with the gun began to step backwards, all the while screaming out commands of, "Stop," and, "Don't come any closer!"

But none of these seemed to stop Joshua's body. He was a train now, a Juggernaut of justice that must find its target and stop any future crime from ever being committed! Joshua's body leaped into the air aimed directly at the mugger, who was now almost completely pressed against the back wall of the alley. As Joshua's body met the muggers, he did not feel flesh first, but steel. A loud crack rang out and bounced off the cement walls, dissipating into the night sky, as the two men began to wrestle. Joshua was struck by the first bullet, and he could feel the air around him growing harder to inhale. Adrenaline took over, however, and the pain was barely noticed.

"This is it," Joshua thought to himself, "I'm a hero, this is my destiny in life!" Two more loud cracks rang out. The mugger reeled back in pain, as he fell to the ground. At the same time, Joshua's body itself went limp, and his head made its own cracking noise as it hit against the hard pavement.

"I've done it. It's all over. I'm a …" he thought, as the hair on the back of his head became wet. The mugger rose to his feet, holding his bloodied leg and limped towards Joshua's now completely incapacitated body. The mugger drew his gun and pointed it between Joshua's eyes.

"It didn't have to go this far, man. I just needed the money! Why did you have to try to be a hero?"

The mugger turned his head, closed his eyes, and breathing heavily, pullied back the trigger. Joshua closed his eyes, waiting to enter that darkness that came with such things as bullets to the head; but the darkness never came.

Out of the entrance of the alleyway stood a tall man whom Joshua could have sworn he had seen before. It's hard to recall names of people you have seen in the past when you are bleeding all over the place.

The tall man charged headfirst into the mugger, spearing him into the brick wall. Joshua heard two more gunshots before he started to fade out of consciousness.

KRAKOW! KRAKOW!

The sound reminded him of the little speech bubbles you see in comic books. In those stories when someone got shot it was always much more epic and romanticized than the real thing. If his twelve year old self could see into the future, he would have burnt his childhood comic books right then and there. The real thing wasn't epic at all; it was brutish and morbid. The last thing he saw before the darkness flooded his eyes, was his white, two-hundred dollar button up shirt, slowly turning candy apple red. Joshua closed his heavy eyes, and let the sound of sirens lull him asleep. As he slept, he dreamed a dream …

Joshua found himself drifting through darkness—expecting to see a tunnel, looking for the light that would ultimately be waiting at the end. He saw nothing. His mind flew to mindless thoughts. He remembered jumping off the dock at summer camp. Splashing down into the shallow lake, and wondering if there really was a monster that lurked deep in the center. He thought of his best friend A-Chan and how he was probably waiting for him at the bar wondering why he was so late. More likely for A-Chan, he was wondering if he was going to get some money out of Joshua tonight. A-Chan always had a way of weaseling out a couple of dollars from his "good old buddy" Joshua; tonight it was going to be his handy dandy dime-bag that would do the trick.

A-Chan had always been "that guy." The sort of friend that is not really a friend but more of a nuisance. He always seemed to have a knack for finding trouble. Even as kids, he and Joshua would break windows together and steal candy from convenience stores. A-Chan didn't have a wealthy father to fall back on like Joshua; instead, he kept on in his life of crime and was always too eager to lead Joshua down the same path.

Joshua's mind kept jumping from thought to thought as he floated aimlessly through the nothingness of this … well, whatever this was. He felt like Alice falling down the rabbit hole. Little did he know just how far this rabbit hole would take him. The falling felt like it would have gone on for all of eternity had he not hit ground and gone unconscious.

And now here he was, stuck in a dark prison cell being held captive by some strange shrouded creature. He may have had no idea what exactly was going on (or how dying in his world had ended him up here), but the one thing he did know was that he needed to find a way out, and fast.

3
FOND MEMORIES

J•OSHUA STRUCK THE WALL with his fist. His fingers throbbed with pain. He could still feel pain … awesome. The room he had been placed in was a prison–a windowless, lifeless, empty, foul-smelling place. Why was he here? What did he ever do to deserve this? Certainly he deserved something better; after all, he had died saving a girl's life! Oh, but how cruel the world was. How hopeless things were. His only hope was to sit and wait; wait to go to whatever hellish place was in store for him once Death had been found. Suddenly, the old Victorian paintings of Hell flashed into his mind and he imagined an eternity of torture, pain, burning and misery. He began to search every corner of the room, frantically looking for a way out. He felt as if he had been searching his whole life for a way out, and, man, wasn't it cruel irony that even in death, he was still searching.

He had grown up in a rich family: a mother who loved tanning more than her children and a father who loved work more than his family. He thought back to the time he had fallen out of his tree fort. A young boy lying half unconscious in the dirt with a huge gash across his forehead. One would assume his mother would be close by, ready to spring into action like a mighty lioness at the slightest whimper from her cub. It was not his mother who ran to his aid. It was his nanny, Roberta. No. His mother was too busy getting her nails done that day, which he learned later, meant that she was having an affair with her "lover," Antony.

Not to put all the blame on her of course, that would be unfair! His father couldn't come to his rescue that day because he was away on business in Columbia. Not that his father was lying; he really was away on business in Columbia. It was just that he was *always* away on business. How many "momentous" occasions had his father missed because of his work? Too many to count, that's for sure.

"Sorry Joshy," they would say, "but you are such a big boy aren't you! You barely even need your mommy or daddy!" Joshua was six at the time. It was at the tender age of thirteen when his parents finally got a divorce. His dad later wished to all the stars in the heavens that he had made his wife sign a prenuptial agreement. Joshua's father didn't grieve long, however. Just a year later, and he had already remarried. This time to a twenty-four year old waitress whom he had taken a liking to. It didn't matter that his dad was fifty-six at the time. Age is blind when large amounts of cash are involved.

"Or how about my brother!" he thought. His older brother Marcus had always been a role model to him. He was a senior in college just as Joshua was beginning his freshman year. He could remember a time when he looked up to his older brother. He would watch him around campus, watch how smooth he was with the ladies, how he would handle the other "tough guys." Joshua wanted to be just like Marcus. Kids would say, "You're Marcus' little brother aren't you?" Joshua would nod. "Yeah man, he's cool. Let him in." And then boom! Instant VIP access, baby. And that's how it was most of the year. Joshua had surprisingly little contact with his brother, and yet, he could use his name alone to get into the coolest parties on campus. It kept up like this until that one fateful night when he and his brother just happened to be at the same party.

A-Chan and Joshua had just arrived when one of Marcus' posse came rushing down the stairs, shoving himself through the front door. The sound of screams poured out from the upstairs bedroom and immediately people began scrambling for the door.

"It's the cops!" a girl's voice cried out. Joshua could still remember how quiet it all seemed despite the chaos as he walked up the now busy stairway. The only thing he could hear was his brother's name being repeated over and over as blue and red lights flashed through the windows and into the darkened house.

Joshua reached the top of the stairs and looked down the long hallway leading into the master bedroom. The door was cracked and the only thing holding it open was a hand that now acted as a doorstop. Joshua walked slowly to the door; his mind racing with thoughts of who it was that was attached to that hand.

"Please don't be Marcus!" he whispered. "Please don't be my brother." He pushed the door wide and saw that the hand belonged to a young girl who was half-naked and motionless. Sitting up against the wall was his brother Marcus. Except this wasn't the calm and cool Marcus. It wasn't the handsome athletic Marcus either. This was overdosed-and-on-the-verge-of-death Marcus.

Joshua fell to his knees speechless. His role model now before him, just a shell of his former self. Marcus glared at Joshua and smiled.

"'Glamorous, ain't it?" he said. These were the last words that Joshua would ever hear his brother speak. The police came stampeding into the room and in a flash, there was a flurry of sirens, handcuffs, and stretchers. Joshua was questioned later at the police station, but he didn't say a word. He just stared at the wall as the officer explained how the young girl was raped and then died from an overdose. The officer thought that Joshua had something to do with it, after all, he was Marcus' little brother. Joshua, who had tried so hard his entire life to be associated with his brother, now wanted nothing to do with him.

He knew that if he ever got the chance to see his brother one-on-one, he would certainly kill him himself for what he had done to that girl; for what he had done to the picturesque image that was now shattered in his head. Kill him for the years of therapy it took for him to get to some semblance of normal after what he had seen. But Joshua would never get the chance. Marcus Hawkins' heart stopped the next day in room three at Ezekiel Thomas Memorial Hospital at 6:26 in the morning.

The paramedic who had answered the call showed up at the funeral along with maybe twenty-five others. The paramedic (sadly enough) was the only person who shed a tear besides Joshua's mother. Joshua's father never showed his face out of shame; it would have been bad for business. Mr. Hawkins, who had never drank in his entire life, could not be found without a drink in his hands for the next few weeks.

And then, out of the blue, everything just went back to normal. Joshua's dad acted as if the entire thing never happened and all the pictures of Marcus "mysteriously" disappeared from around the house. The ex-Mrs. Hawkins never mentioned him either, and for Joshua that was all too welcome. Marcus' name became taboo around the family. Saying his name became equivalent to mentioning the Nazis around German people. It just wasn't polite.

"None of this is fair!" Joshua screamed out into the cell. "I didn't ask for this life! I didn't ask for the cards that I was dealt. I just had to survive! If you can hear me, God, or whatever, this isn't my fault!"

He pounded the side of the walls with his fists. The chains on his wrists rattled against the cell and echoed violently throughout the room. His head split with the sound of it and he fell down to his knees once more. The sound of metal-on-metal reminded him of the Ghost of Christmas past from *The Christmas Carol*. Sitting down, Joshua thought of how unfair that story was. Why did Scrooge get warnings in life that he was on the wrong path? Where were my three freakin' ghosts?! If there was a God, somewhere, He certainly wasn't a fair one! God set my up for failure, and now He sits on His throne just laughing about the entire thing.

Back on earth, he would not be missed. He was certain of it. He could see his obituary now:

Joshua Hawkins was twenty-five years old, a young vice-president for his father's clothing company, Avarice, and had every opportunity to live the American Dream. Joshua leaves behind nobody who cares about him. He didn't even have a girlfriend, sad, yes? Joshua Hawkins was twenty-five years old ... twenty-five years old and dead.

Good riddance!

4

A PRISON OF THE MIND

THE DARKNESS OF JOSHUA'S PRISON began to take on a life of its own. It started to feel as if he was swimming through molasses. Claustrophobia was setting in. He swiped at the air, searching for the walls, feeling around looking for a weak point or fracture, but found nothing. He even tried screaming for help. Nobody came. No big surprise there. The screams echoed in his steel cell. He screamed until his throat felt as if it was on the verge of bleeding. He was helpless. He had been alone in life, and now he was alone in death. Joshua thought once more of how much this prison was like his life; of how the only people who might notice he was gone were the owners of the local liquor store. Joshua stared into the void of his prison and wept (something he had not done in years).

A few hours passed, or what seemed like hours (who could really be sure in a place like this?) when something began stirring behind Joshua's head. The steel cell was vibrating ever so slightly. The walls were made of metal, thus, any vibration or sound would set them off in a frenzy of movement. The source of the vibration was a small sound coming from outside the cell.

"A voice?" he thought. "Skinless must be returning to take me with him."

The vibrating started slowly, becoming more intense with each passing second. He pressed his ear up against the cold metal and listened carefully. He could hear the noise becoming more and more audible as whoever (or whatever) was drawing closer. The voice outside was singing. Strange. Even stranger was the fact that

Joshua thought he actually recognized the song. Where had he heard it before?

He wracked his brain to remember the melody, suddenly, it came to him. He had been standing outside his father's office building, smoking a cigar, when the doors of the church across the street had opened for a brief second. Joshua had muttered some joke about the Pope walking into a bar under his breath but thought the music was beautiful nonetheless. Something about the music had scared him, however. Yes, it was pleasant, but the words, something about the words, had made him uneasy. The same feeling of uneasiness came over him now as the voice outside the cell became louder and much clearer:

> "It was a strange and dreadful strife
> when life and death contended;
> The victory remained with life;
> the reign of death was ended.
> Stripped of power, no more it reigns,
> an empty form alone remains
> Death's sting is lost forever! Alleluia!"

The voice appeared to be right outside the door now, singing its terrifying song. Joshua fell into a fetal position covering his ears as the oscillating clamor became so intense that he thought the cell might explode. He fixed his eyes on the door, waiting anxiously for Skinless to burst through it and drag him into an eternity of regrets. As Joshua rolled in the dark, he closed his eyes in hopelessness, crying out his final plea.

"Help me, please, someone, anyone! Take me from this place of misery, I want another chance!" And with those words, the vibrating of the prison stopped.

"Who's in there?" The being from outside spoke with a deep resonating voice; a voice which, oddly enough, soothed Joshua. The voice was like a mother's hug which dries the tears of a crying child. Joshua wondered if perhaps this was some sick trick to frighten him or make him even more vulnerable than he already was.

"Skinless, I know it's you out there! Just come inside and get this over with! Stop your stupid mind games!" Tears poured down his face, intermingled with his sweat, making a nice salty cocktail.

Joshua waited for a response. For a few seconds, there was nothing but silence. Suddenly, the voice spoke; a voice so tender and yet so fierce that all the love and strength in the world could be heard in it.

"Do not be afraid, I am not Skinless, but I do know of him. Hold on, and I will release you from your prison."

Joshua remained curled up in a ball, afraid to move. The unknown being's voice had him paralyzed. It was as if he were under a spell. In the back of his mind he hoped it was Skinless at the door. The new voice frightened him more than that of his captor's. The wheel on the metal door began to move. That old familiar beam of light shone through the opening and blinded Joshua. He threw himself back and swatted at the floating dots in front of his eyes.

Joshua's vision cleared, and looking up, he saw the silhouette of a man standing in the doorway. It was not the emaciated, shrouded figure of Skinless, but a man, six feet tall, maybe more, wearing a robe made of white. His hair was long and flowing down to his hips. His beard was dreaded and gray. Joshua spoke with a strange courage that had all of a sudden overcome him.

"Who are you, and what do you want with me?"

"My name is Apostolos, I have been sent to be your guide."

"My guide?" Joshua laughed. "Thanks, but no thanks. The last guy who offered to be my guide wanted to take me to Hell, which, up until this point, I didn't even think existed. Where do you want to take me, the North Pole?"

There was desperation in Joshua's voice, he was going insane, and he felt it. He caught himself, and tried to be more civil; more human.

"I'm sorry, thanks for opening the door and everything, but I would just as soon leave and be on my way by myself. I don't need a guide. I will find my own way out of this place. Why don't you take my advice and get out of here before Skinless returns and captures us both?"

The man called Apostolos walked towards Joshua–who had now made it to a kneeling position–and bent down. He placed his hand behind Joshua's neck and spoke. His voice was soft and kind and Joshua felt as if cold water was being poured over his head.

"Joshua, for twenty-five years, you lived without a purpose. You fed every sickening desire and became a slave to the flesh. You followed your own path all of your life, and ended it as a disgraceful stain on society, even a stain on the cement where you died. You were chosen Joshua, thus, I have come to show you a path out of this place. You will fight my words at first, because you do not understand them. I tell you the truth, Joshua, you were meant for great things; much greater things than to be the savior of a girl in an alleyway who will never know your name. Your heart knows my words are true. Leave your prison, Joshua. My Master has opened the door. All you have to do is walk through it and follow the path before you."

Joshua's heart knew these words. He knew them all too well for he had frequented churches all of his life...on holidays that is. His "new" mom liked to attend candlelight services and such on special occasions. This type of jargon was commonly heard at mass and the like, and for Joshua, commonly slept through. He resisted the temptation to doze off this time. He had too many questions for this strange man to do so.

"Are you Christ–that is to say–are you Jesus?" Joshua asked.

"You speak names of power, Joshua. You speak my Master's name. That Name is above all names and with it comes all the power in the world, for my Master holds the world in the palm of His hand. Joshua, do you long to release yourself from those shackles on your wrists and ankles? My King alone holds the keys to life and salvation from the place which you are headed. How long will you continue in your old ways? My Master is preparing a place for you, Joshua. Follow His path, and you shall find a dwelling in his household."

Apostolos smiled. His eyes were like blue fire blazing in the darkness. He helped Joshua to his feet, led him into the beam of light coming from the door, and placed his arm around his shoulder.

"It's a beautiful day isn't it Joshua? A day like this comes once in a million years. I had a day like this once, and I missed it. Don't miss your day."

"What do you mean by that? Don't miss my day?" Joshua asked.

"I thought you wanted to go your own way Joshua? What more can a foolish old man say to such a bright young man as yourself?" Apostolos gave a small laugh and smiled.

"If it pleases you, and I must be quick, I will show you of how I came to be in this place."

Joshua, not quite ready to be rid of this man's company after having been couped up all alone in a cell for so long, thought that he would indulge the "old timer."

"Why not. It's not as if I have anything else better to do at the moment. I mean, I'm dead. I have all the time in the world right?"

Apostolos smiled once more.

"This may feel like a rush of blood to the head. Try not to pass out." Apostolos reached his hand out and placed it on Joshua's forehead.

"Umm, yeah … what are you doi …" Joshua didn't even get a chance to finish his sentence. Before he knew it, the tale of Apostolos was swimming in his brain.

5
I Who Speak to You Am He

"COME, SEE A MAN who told me everything I ever did!" cried a voice.

Caleb stirred in his bed as a women's voice came whisking through his window as if it were carried on the breeze. He grabbed a washcloth and rubbed the sweat off his face. Before he was awakened, he was having an extremely vivid dream, in which his camel was talking to him and asking him for some wine. He decided as he washed his face that he was spending far too much time out in the heat. With dreams like this he knew he needed some time off.

"Come, everyone! See a man who told me everything I ever did!"

The voice came to his ears once more. What he at first had thought was just a part of his dream had become a reality to him. He got up, cracked his back and walked over to the window. He looked down at the usually quiet town of Sychar, which at the present was now in an uproar. Men and women were running through the streets muttering things to each other. The leaders of the town had gathered around a lone woman and were listening intently to what she was saying.

Caleb grabbed his robe, covered himself and headed outside to discover the source of all the commotion. He pushed past a few people here and there on the street and headed towards the town elders.

"Do you know what's happening?" he stopped to ask a food vendor.

"No idea," he replied, "some lady just came rushing through town screaming that she had met some prophet or something."

Caleb continued on towards the large crowd that had now amassed itself around the woman. He squeezed his way through the crowd until he was only a few feet away from the elders and the woman.

"Slow down and tell us what has happened." One of the elders grabbed the woman by the shoulder and tried to calm her down.

"A prophet has come to us!" she said. "He spoke to me and told me everything I ever did. He knows things about me, even though we have never met. Please, you must come with me and meet Him. Could this be the Messiah?" With the mention of the Messiah, the crowd excitedly talked amongst themselves.

The elders of the town broke off from the crowd and huddled together. They were in deep discussion. Some of the old ones threw their hands up in the air, while the younger ones would turn red in the face at times–holding back words.

After a few minutes of fevered debate, they turned back around and approached the now even larger crowd.

"Alright," they said, "take us to this prophet you have told us about, and we will judge for ourselves."

The woman led the sizable crowd to Jacob's Well where she had met the man. Some turned away and went back to work, while others dropped what they were doing to go be a part of the excitement. Caleb just watched in disbelief as they followed after the woman.

"How could they believe anything a woman like that says? And to mention the Messiah?! Who does she think she is putting hope in their hearts like that?"

Caleb was a Samaritan whose father was a Jew but had intermarried. He was about thirty-four years old and had been married once, but his wife had died young. He had long, flowing brown hair and a beard of which he was very proud. It was not easy being thirty-four and a widower at such a young age. Furthermore, as the son of a Jew who had married a Samaritan, it made Caleb a "half-breed"; an outcast.

His father saw to it that he memorized the Scriptures backwards and forwards. He knew all about the promised Messiah, the prophecies, and the warnings against false prophets. This woman was nothing more than one of them. He headed back towards his house, opened the door and immediately went back to bed. Again, he found himself looking his camel in the face while it pleaded with him for more wine.

"You're a camel!" he kept yelling, but the camel would simply reply, "And you're a human, now give me more wine!"

The elders arrived at the well and found the man of which the woman spoke. Through His words and wonders, He was proven to be a prophet by the elders and was asked if he would stay with them for two days. Caleb purposely avoided that side of town and even tried to steer clear of the gossipers who lurked around every corner waiting anxiously to tell anyone who would listen about this man called Jesus. Caleb thought nothing of this Jesus. He heard that he was born in Nazareth, was the son of a carpenter and was definitely not a warrior king. All good Jews knew the Messiah would be someone that everyone would know. He would be royalty, and he would be a warrior king. The Messiah would be someone who would destroy the Romans and bring forth Shalom; someone like David.

Caleb wanted nothing to do with false prophets or the rumors that surrounded them. He continued on with his business, and with the passing of time, the man, Jesus left the town of Sychar.

As the years passed by, the town changed. The man Jesus had been killed by the Romans and Jews on charges of heresy, and in Caleb's eyes, justice had been served. Many, however, (including Sychar) still believed that this Jesus had been the Messiah. Caleb would say, "Isn't our Messiah supposed to stop the Romans? Instead, this impostor was killed by them and even rejected by *his* own people. That *man,* was not our Messiah."

The people who heard this would argue that Jesus had resurrected, and would one day return. Caleb didn't want to hear any more of this nonsense, and so he lived in his own town like a hermit. He stayed close to home; only coming out to tend to his field and trade with the other merchants. He did not live like this for long; however, for another man who spoke words of power came walking into town a few months after Jesus' death.

A traveler, Paul, came preaching the scriptures. He spoke Caleb's language, the words of the prophets, men like Isaiah, words he understood. Paul set himself up a place to speak in the middle of town, and most everyone came out to hear his message—even Caleb. Paul broke down the scriptures and pulled out the prophecies concerning the man Jesus. Caleb listened intently, quoting the scriptures in his mind right along with Paul. Paul would take a passage and then explain how it pointed to Jesus being the Messiah. He did this over and over again for hours, and finally he delivered the knockout punch. He explained why Jesus died and linked it back to Isaiah's prophecies.

Caleb was floored by Paul's words. After he was finished speaking, Caleb invited him to his house. Paul stayed for a few days, and by the time he stepped out the door Caleb had sold his things and was following after him. Caleb was a changed man. He was now a follower of Jesus: a Christian.

Caleb spent a year with Paul; learning from him and helping him spread the gospel message. After the year had passed, Paul sent Caleb out on his own to preach. Caleb was a powerful speaker, and he had a powerful message.

"Come, see a man who told me everything I ever did." He would tell of the woman at the well and how Jesus had spoken to her as if He knew her entire life. He would tell of how his only regret in life was that he missed his chance to see his Savior face-to-face. Oh, how he longed to see his Savior's face.

Caleb went from town-to-town spreading the good news, and after a few years, he had become quite well known. He boarded a boat headed for Rome and started spreading the message of Jesus in that region as well. Most took to the message quite well. The Romans however, would mock him; calling him Apostolos, which in Greek means "Apostle." They would call him this because they knew he had missed his chance to see Jesus.

Around this time, the Roman Emperor was persecuting Christians mercilessly. The Emperor wanted to go back to the old gods; the old ways, and he saw the Christian God as a threat. Each day, he gathered hundreds of Christians and threw them to the wild beasts in the Coliseum. Caleb and others like him were rushed into hiding by their followers. It was not long before each of the well-known Christians were rounded up and thrown to the lions one-by-one.

Caleb managed to stay hidden for quite some time, and with each passing day the Emperor grew more furious. He would get reports of secret meetings and of his own men converting to Christianity because of the one they called "Apostolos." He now directed his full attention to catching this outlaw. He arranged for one of his most trusted men to pretend to be interested in joining the Jesus sect. The plan was that once he was in and had found out where they met, he would alert his men and rush in to capture Caleb.

It took the soldier three weeks to discover the whereabouts of the Christian meetings. He gathered up his men and surrounded the building. The soldiers rushed in and slaughtered the entire house except Caleb. They murdered not only the men and women, but the children as well.

"The only good Christian is a dead Christian," the soldier said as he wiped his blade and tied up Caleb.

They took Caleb straight to the Emperor and placed him, gagged and bound, at his feet.

"Untie him," the Emperor smirked a smirk that only evil men's faces have the capacity to do. The Emperor's men cut the ropes from Caleb's arms and feet and removed his gag.

"Well, well, if it isn't the famous Apostolos," the Emperor scoffed. "The man whose words taste like honey, and whose voice calms even the most ferocious of beasts. Perhaps these rumors are true! You may very well ride one of my lions out of the arena tomorrow!" The men all burst out laughing as the Emperor threw himself backwards in his chair, holding his stomach at the "hilarious" joke he had just made. Caleb stayed on his knees with his eyes closed and his hands clasped.

"Apostolos, have you nothing to say?" the Emperor said growing more and more agitated by the second. "Perhaps you are too busy praying to your God for deliverance? Well, I am waiting. Where is your God now? Where was He when your precious Jesus was killed?" Caleb remained quiet. "Can you not answer these questions? Can you not overpower me and my men and run me through with my very own sword? Surely your God has that power, no?"

Caleb stayed still, hands still clasped, eyes still closed. Silence swept over the room. The Emperor rose from his chair, walked forward to the motionless Apostolos, and spit in his face.

"Guards, get this dog out of my—"

"My Emperor," Apostolos said, the spit sliding down his left cheek, "I do not pray for safety. I pray that my God has mercy on your men for the innocent lives they have taken this night."

"My men? You pray for my men? You really are too much! I will enjoy watching your flesh get torn from your bones tomorrow. Get him out of here!" The Emperor thrust out his arm, motioning the guards to remove Caleb from his presence.

Once again, Caleb was tied and gagged and led down to the prison with the other Christians. The guards took their time roughing him up a bit.

"Oh, our sweet Father!" said one of the guards, kneeling in front of Apostolos. "Please save our dear brother Apostolos from the beating of which he is about to receive." The guards kicked until their legs grew tired, and boredom set in. Caleb didn't say a word.

The sun set and the sun arose.

The crowd shuffled into the Coliseum and the games began. Caleb and the others waited behind a large iron gate as the sound of jeers and clapping thundered around them.

The gates burst open and the Christians toppled out, struggling over each other as sweat and spit flew from their bodies. One of the elderly was crushed beneath the weight of the flailing Christians, and they scattered as the crowd looked down laughing and hissing.

The Emperor sat high above from his throne, watching them like ants grasping at the walls trying to climb out of their circular prison.

"If you will but renounce your Christ and turn to the gods of old, your life will be spared this day!" the Emperor's voice boomed out across the arena, as the people cheered at his words. Some of the Christians ran up to the wall and cried out to him. They declared the Emperor as lord, and swore allegiance to the old gods. The Emperor's guards rushed in and grabbed the few mutinous Christians, as the others watched mournfully as the ones they called brothers and sisters left them behind to die.

The gates closed once more, and the Emperor looked at the few remaining Christians and thrust his arm forward. He stood and turned his thumb sideways. The crowd hushed as they waited for the verdict. They knew what was going to happen, but they wanted the rush that came with the downward thumb. The Emperor did not disappoint this day; his thumb came down like a crooked judge's gavel. The gates rose as the starved lions came springing forth. The Christians scattered, as mothers grabbed children and husbands grabbed wives. Caleb watched helplessly as the lions devoured his brothers and sisters. The sun beat down and the crowd grew louder as if fueled by its rays.

Caleb dashed towards the Emperor's wall and threw himself down in front of him. The Emperor stood and walked to the edge, waiting for the mighty Apostolos to cry out his allegiance to Rome, and deny his Christ before the masses. Caleb fell headfirst before the Emperor and breathed deeply the blood soaked dirt that covered the arena floor. He could almost hear the cries of thousands, the cries of the righteous calling out from the dirt. He lifted himself to his knees and looked up into the face of the Emperor.

"My Lord! My Lord!" he gasped as he cried out these words, clearly, and deeply moved with agony of spirit. The Emperor grinned, waiting for Apostolos to utter those last few words and have his men rush in and do what Apostolos' God could not.

"My Lord, make this quick so that I might live in disgrace no longer. Forgive me for not believing that woman, and forgive this man who stands before me!"

As Caleb closed his mouth, the lion's mouth opened and shut around his head. In the darkness, he thought of one thing and one thing only.

"Finally, I will see my Savior's face at last."

A headless body falls to the dirt and the one they call Apostolos is no more.

The Emperor stumbles backwards, his face twisted with anger. He hates these Christians, hates them so much. He sits back down in his chair and seethes with anger. Somewhere deep down, he feels something else that he loathes as well. He is envious of their faith.

6

A FORK IN THE ROAD, A KNIFE IN THE BACK

POSTOLOS REMOVED HIS HAND from Joshua's forehead like an old televangelist, and as he did, Joshua tumbled backwards into the cell.

"Now you know my story. I figured it was only fair considering I know yours. You are the girl at the well, Joshua. My Master knows everything that you have ever done, and yes, He still wants to welcome you to His house. Now get out of this cell, don't miss your chance to meet Him. Haven't you been in bondage long enough?"

Apostolos helped the young man up, and started for the door.

"Oh, one last thing Joshua, and this is extremely important. You must take the narrow path, for the wide one leads to destruction. You are not alone my friend. Farewell!"

Apostolos vanished just as quickly and mysteriously as he had come. Joshua stared at the open door afraid of what awaited him outside, but even more afraid at the way his heart now felt.

Had evangelists on TV been right all those years? Was the one they called Jesus in his world and this world? Better yet, where was this world? Was it all in his head? Apostolos mentioned Heaven. That was God's place. Skinless, well he mentioned Hell. That was the red-suited pitchfork guy's home; the Devil's place.

Joshua knew the basics, but he just thought it was all mumbo-jumbo. How could you prove any of it? Certainly not with science, and that whole faith thing had never been his cup o' tea. Now he was faced with two truths: Hell on one path and Heaven on the other. His decision seemed simple. Heaven is the easy choice, right? But how many fools have thought this same thing and ended up in the eternal pit?

Joshua stood up and made his way towards the door–his chains now heavier perhaps. With each step his heart pounded faster. It was like he was back at home during Christmas, and this door was his biggest present. What would be behind the wrapping he wondered? Probably coal. He had been a very naughty boy. He reached for the wheel on the metal door (which had somehow closed shut after Apostolos' disappearing act), and pulled it open. Light poured into the empty cell like a flood of water, so that no darkness remained. Joshua was free.

Stepping through the doorway, Joshua breathed deeply, like a swimmer resurfacing from the depths; like a child emerging from the womb. This was his first breath ever; his breath of life.

He looked around and surveyed this strange new world. It was very much like his world. Trees, grass, sky, except everything was slightly off. The sky was a light shade of purple, and cloudless. The trees were full of leaves, but they all looked dead, and the grass was a patchy dark orange.

He was in a field of sorts. The prison in which he had been locked up reminded him of a metal storage crate like the ones you might find on big ocean freighters. He looked around and saw what must have been thousands, no, millions of similar crates. Perhaps others just like him were trapped inside waiting to be freed, but that was none of his concern. The whole reason he was in this mess in the first place was because he tried to save someone. From now on, he would worry about himself. Leave the rescuing to Apostolos and his Master.

He looked to the left of his cell and could clearly see a narrow cobblestone path leading into a very dark forest filled with even more dead-leafed trees. To the right was a wide road made of asphalt that led to what looked like a large city off in the distance. A heavy fog was rolling in, and knowing that he would soon lose sight of both paths, a decision must be made, and quick.

"Fine, Apostolos," he said, "I made the first step, now what? That creepy forest?"

A loud bang like a shotgun blast hit Joshua from behind, and he was knocked forward onto his face. Spitting grass and struggling to wipe dirt out of his eyes with the chains around his wrists, he staggered to his feet. Swinging around quickly, he realized his cell had completely vanished. Lying on the ground where the cell had been was a piece of paper. Joshua walked over, picked it up and began to read:

Joshua Hawkins,

You are cordially invited to the city of Lovelight! Take the wide path, for the narrow one is a long road fraught with peril. Few travel that way, and I'm afraid the path has become quite overgrown with thorns. We are eagerly awaiting your arrival. See you soon!

Your friend,
Lanirche

Joshua read the piece of paper once, twice, and even a third time.

"Who the heck is Lanirche?" he asked himself. "And how did he know I would be here?"

Joshua was starting to grow uneasy about the entire thing. Before reading the note, he had already decided in his mind that the city would be the best bet despite what Apostolos had said, but now, well, he wasn't so sure. Still, the forest was completely creepy in every sense of the word. Whenever he looked in the direction of the forest, he felt like it was looking back at him. The city was starting to look more appealing by the second.

"Besides, that city is probably filled with people who can help me," Joshua reasoned.

But even as Joshua pondered these things, a sense of uncertainty began to grow inside him. Something was different about Joshua but he didn't know it yet. He was changing, and that feeling of wrongdoing was growing into something he had always just chosen not to listen to; a conscience; a counselor.

Joshua stood at a fork in the road. He folded the paper up and put it into his back pocket. He stepped onto the asphalt and headed towards the city. The road was badly beaten and worn. You could tell by the divots and potholes that this highway was heavily traveled. As he walked, he passed a sign that read:

CITY OF LOVELIGHT
WE HAVE EVERYTHING.
ALL THAT'S MISSING IS YOU!

Lovelight was the name strangers knew the town by, but all the residents knew it by another name. They all called it Pandemonium.

7
A Tragedy Observed

MEANWHILE, IN AN APARTMENT BUILDING back in Chicago ...

"Reuben, quick call 911, there's somebody down in the alleyway hurt!"

Reuben, a fifty-seven year old overweight man who had not done anything quick for quite some time ran ... waddled to the phone. His wife was screaming at the window, staring down into the alley from the fifth story of their apartment building. Reuben fumbled with the phone, he realized how scared he was to actually call 911, after all, everyone knows the number, but who in their life actually finds a reason to dial it? His chubby fingers smashing at the buttons, resulting in two buttons being pressed at once.

"I'm sorry, please hang up and try again," a robotic voice replied.

"Dagnabbit!" cried Reuben, as he put the phone down on the receiver and tried again.

"Hello, 911, what is the nature of your emergency?" a calm women's voice came across the other line of the receiver.

"Yes, my wife just witnessed a shooting in the alleyway outside our apartment building. We heard gunshots! Someone's not moving down there! Hurry!"

"Okay, sir, just remain calm," said the operator, in her cool, collected voice. "What is the address from which you are calling?"

"We are in an apartment building, Judge's Suites, yeah that's right. It's off of 1st and Nun Blvd."

Reuben tried to remain focused while his wife issued commands from across the room.

"Okay, sir," said the operator, "we will send an ambulance and police cars right away, please stay on the line until they arrive."

"Reuben, the shooter is running and I think he's being chased by someone! Oh heavens! Maybe it's an undercover cop!" his wife clearly excited now had her face firmly pressed against the glass window.

"Ma'am, my wife is telling me the shooter is being chased by a man. The police need to be careful. That alleyway is a dead end and they don't want to shoot the wrong guy!"

"Yes, sir," the operator's voice stayed calm, cool, and collected. This wasn't her first rodeo. "I will notify the officers immediately of the situation."

KRAKOW, KRAKOW! ... the sound of two shots fired came from the alleyway below. Reuben froze in his shoes as his wife fainted and fell to the floor. He immediately dropped the phone and ran to her side.

"Sir, what was that? What's going on? Please remain calm, sir. Are you still there? Is everything okay?" the operator spoke to no one, as the phone dangled by its cord. Her voice this time not as Fonzie-esque as before.

Reuben picked up his wife and laid her down on the sofa, he ran back and grabbed the phone from its hangman position, as more gunshots rattled from the alley below.

"Oh my word, they're all dead! All three of them down there, dead."

Reuben held the phone to his ear. His face perspiring from the recent dead-lift of his wife. His eyes widened as he looked through the window. Staring at not just one body, but three. Three bodies motionless. Three bodies bleeding. Three sons, three brothers; three bodies. Reuben slid down to his cold wooden floor and crawled to the couch. He held his wife in his arms as the sound of sirens came near. She had never looked so beautiful, and he had never loved her as much as he did now. "Life is short," he thought, "life is too short".

8
THE ROAD TO HELL IS PAVED WITH GREAT ADVERTISEMENTS

J•OSHUA WALKED DOWN THE ASPHALT ROAD, careful to avoid the holes that littered its way. As he walked, he saw the city skyline grow closer. He started to notice large billboards advertising all sorts of products. These were products from his world but all with different names. One looked like it might be for a brand of cigarettes that were called "Small Delights." Another for a beer company called "Barley Pops" depicting a child (probably no more than twelve) holding a bottle, smiling.

Every mile or so, however, there was one billboard that would repeat itself. This billboard was advertising what looked like a lawyer's office. The word "Lanirche" was posted above the man's head in big neon letters. The man's smile seemed to hide something, but Joshua didn't know what. It was almost as if this man's image was staring into his very soul – as if it were calling to him.

"Keep up the pace Joshua," the face said, "You are almost home."

Joshua felt a chill come over him as he gazed into Lanirche's vacant smile.

"Lanirche?" he thought. Reaching into his back pocket, Joshua pulled out the letter he had found on the ground near his cell. Skipping to the bottom, he recalled the name.

"Must be the guy who sent me this letter," he guessed. "If he is a lawyer or whatever, maybe he can help me out in this 'world'. Or, at least maybe he can get this Skinless guy off my back."

The idea did seem rather foolish. However, so did the idea of a thousand year old evangelist, an ominous shrouded creature, and God and the Devil fighting for his soul. Yeah, at this point, even the foolish ideas sounded epic.

Joshua pulled himself away from the billboard and moved on, drawing ever closer to the bright city lights. The light outside was starting to diminish. Joshua looked upward, thinking maybe the sun was starting to set. That would have been the case had he remembered ever seeing a sun. The light here didn't seem to have a source. It didn't feel right; it felt fake, wrong, evil.

The sound of a busy city came to his ears, and with it the thoughts of the light fell into the back of his mind as he was reminded of Chicago. He was immediately transported, in his mind, back home. He pictured himself walking down those bubblegum covered streets once more–seeing "Wild Bill" the curbside prophet being wonderfully crazy as he passed by. The sounds of the city buzzed through his ears and struck his brain like a horde of angry bees. He started into a full on run now towards the city, excited at the prospect of being "home" (or at least a place much like home) once again.

As he got closer, however, he didn't hear the sound of car horns. He didn't smell hotdogs and that usual scent of body odor that comes from cramming too many people in one place. What he did smell, were rotten eggs and something that reminded him of a campfire he once sat around as he and his friends told ghost stories. He heard the sound of many voices, perhaps talking (or was it screaming?). All Joshua knew was that he needed answers. He needed to be free of his chains (the chains that got heavier with each step), and he needed to find out the truth about Apostolos' Master.

"May the truth set me free!" Joshua laughed these words out, unaware that all the while he was headed for the city of lies.

9
ENTER LANIRCHE

SKINLESS WALKS ALONG A NARROW CORRIDOR leading to an elevator. Entering, he hears the sound of an anemic song drizzling out of the overhead speaker. He pushes the button for the 666th floor, and hums the song nervously as the elevator rises. Seconds pass, and soon the elevator gurgles out what might have at one time been a lovely chime. He walks out into a dimly lit room. A receptionist sits behind a desk fixing her makeup. The woman's face has been burned horribly, and what isn't burned is pale white; almost as if she has never experienced the sun. Skinless nods to the receptionist as he takes a seat.

"Lanirche is busy at the moment," she squawks. "He will see you shortly."

Skinless stands, bows, and then returns to his seat. The sound of bones cracking can be heard as the shrouded figure lowers itself onto the chair. He sits anxiously, afraid to tell his master that the one named Joshua has escaped; afraid because his master probably already knows.

He sits for an hour or so, and just before he can doze off, the receptionist calls out his name.

"Mr. Skinless," she shrieks, sounding more like a bird than a woman, "Lanirche will see you now."

Skinless stands, moves toward the red door which leads into Lanirche's office and almost wishes he could pray. He opens the door and enters into a dark room. The walls are lined with bookshelves, all of which are chock full of classic works of literature. "The Picture of Dorian Gray" catches Skinless' eye as he looks from side-to-side, doing everything in his power to avoid the man sitting behind the desk at the back of the room. Skinless arrives at his dreaded destination, and bows low before the desk.

"You wanted to see me, master?" Skinless asks.

"Yes, come in, Aleister," said Lanirche, "and take off that hood. No need to hide your hideous appearance from me." Lanirche's voice is cool and amiable. He sits behind a large marble desk, and leans back in his chair as his sparkling white teeth peek out from under his upper lip. He is a young man, perhaps mid-twenties. He has long blond hair which he wears up in a ponytail, and sparkling blue eyes. He wears a tailored suit, and if he were to open up the left side of his jacket, we would see that it was made by the clothing company *Avarice*.

Skinless removes his hood hesitantly and a skull partially covered in flesh is seen. The skin is constantly being fed upon by what appears to be blue flames. They burn what little flesh is left and then it reappears moments later. The face seems sorrowful as if he is in continual pain. His body reeks of rotten eggs and vomit.

"I had forgotten how hideous you actually are, Aleister!" Lanirche says roaring with laughter. He composes himself, and motions his hand towards Skinless. "On second thought, you better put the hood back on."

Lanirche lets out a few more small chuckles as Skinless quickly (and gratefully) pulls back on his hood as he bows before Lanirche.

"I'm sure you know why you're here, don't you, Aleister?" Lanirche asked.

"Master, I am sorry. I had no idea Apostolos would get to him, and besides, I thought after we killed his leader, he would give up the ghost like the rest of them did. Surely you can remember how I persuaded many of His devoted to turn from their foolish beliefs. You must have mercy on me! Besides, there is no need to worry, master; the Prophet is gone, thanks to Death. Joshua will soon lose hope and fall just like the others."

"Never speak of the Prophet in my presence again!" Lanirche's voice changes into a deep guttural yell, and Skinless is sent sprawling backwards at the power of it.

"You have failed me most horribly this time, Aleister. I put up with you because in your time on earth you did some fantastic things, but this kind of lackadaisical attitude must be dealt with. I trusted Death to finish off the One. I trusted him with a plan that I had been devising for years. Now, Death has gone missing, and the One still lives. If that wasn't bad enough, now Apostolos is running around releasing my prisoners! You will be punished severely for this Aleister, and after your punishment, you will hunt down this escapee and continue your search for Death!"

"But sir, I had no idea that the One still lived. If I had known that I would have been —"

Skinless frantically tries to argue for some sort of forgiveness but finds none. The young man behind the desk gives him a glare that quickly shuts him up. Lanirche reaches for a button on his desk and speaks into the microphone attached.

"Linda, tell Vlad that Aleister will be down shortly for some much needed time in the Abyss. Also, get Mammon on the phone. I want to go over our weekly budget."

"Yes sir," the receptionist's voice flutters from the speaker.

Skinless bows once more and turns back toward the door. His knee bones clack together as he walks. Linda, the receptionist, stares on with a frown as Skinless heads into the elevator and presses the very last button which is clearly labeled, "Mr. Vlad's Office". Skinless has been to the Abyss before. He remembers it clearly. You don't ever forget the Abyss. Nobody does.

10

They Call it Pandemonium

J•OSHUA APPROACHED THE CITY WALL and reached a very wide gate that had to be at least four-hundred feet tall. The door was connected to walls that seemed to go on forever in both directions, and the name Mulciber was engraved into the giant metal hinges that held the door in place. He stared up at this monstrosity and wondered what he should do–knock? The sounds of the voices he had heard must have been all in his imagination, because now that he was close he couldn't hear anything; in fact, it was quiet ... dead quiet.

He walked towards the gate, and as he got closer, he saw a sign nailed to the massive wooden structure. He couldn't read the sign, however. It was printed in some foreign language that he had never seen before. Joshua reached out his hand to knock, and just as he moved his fist forward to rap the door, it creaked open a few inches as if it had moved by some unknown force or pressure. The chains around his wrist swung forward and came rushing back, hitting him in the gut, knocking the wind out of him.

Joshua recovered and stared through the crack of the massive door. He saw what looked like an old, abandoned business of some kind. The windows were boarded up, and the sign hanging above tarnished and swinging loosely. It was now night, and the rest of the city was too hard to make out in the present darkness. It didn't help that the city street lights were flickering on and off. Just as his eyes would adjust, another would go out. Joshua decided after a few tedious minutes of contemplating his navel, to step through the massive gate. He would step through as so many had before him.

Joshua carefully slipped his right foot through the crack as if dipping his toes into a pool to make sure the water wasn't too cold. He waited … nothing happened. He called out into the darkness, "Hello, anyone there!?" Once more. "Can anyone hear me!?" Nothing.

Joshua pulled the rest of his body through the crack. No sooner had he done this than the monolithic door came swinging violently shut. Joshua quickly turned and banged on the door, immediately regretting his decision to enter. There was no way a mere mortal could open this door alone.

"Was Apostolos right after all?" he wondered. "Should I have taken the other path?" He could hear two voices telling him two different things. On the right shoulder he imagined a tiny Apostolos in his robe, and on the left, he imagined a miniature Lanirche in his custom-tailored suit.

Tiny Lanirche: "Anyone who has followers that beg for money on television and act all self-righteous on the streets can't be legit."

Losing his mind Joshua: "But Apostolos is different than all the 'Christians' I have ever met in my life. Maybe this whole 'Jesus' thing is also different."

But what he had said wasn't true. He had met a "Christian" much like Apostolos once before. He thought back to one of the times when he had to fly out of the states on a "business trip" for his father. He only went on these trips because he was given free access to the company credit card. Surprisingly, the company's accountants never asked him what all of the "miscellaneous" expenses were. This one particular trip had stuck out to him though.

On the plane, he had sat next to a man who was reading his Bible. Joshua had asked him what that whole Jesus thing was about, and instead of a self-righteous answer like he had expected (like he had wanted), the man simply looked at him and said, "For the most part, love."

"Love," Joshua thought. "That was the answer the guy gave me."

All of his life, he had heard it was just a bunch of works and rules. Christianity wasn't fun, and it definitely wasn't love. I mean, you couldn't even "make love" as a Christian until you were married –lame. He had heard that you had to do X amount of good deeds to get into heaven and then some old guy on a throne welcomed you in and you were set for eternity.

But this guy, man … this guy sat the entire two hour trip and told Joshua all about this Jesus fellow who had died to save sinners, and how He did it because He loved everyone. The guy went on to say that it was nothing he did to deserve it but that it was this free gift of love. Joshua nodded off here and there, but he had heard the gist of it. This was so radically different from everything he had seen on TV and heard in the churches that he had visited. He could still remember the man's face, kind and old. He smelled like Polo, and he had two kids, or was it three? Walter was his name…yeah, Walter.

Joshua's heart swelled at the remembrance of Walter's words, and he felt a sense of regret for disobeying Apostolos. If a man like Apostolos followed Jesus and could walk freely in this horrid place, then maybe the Prophet's path was indeed the only way.

Tiny Apostolos: "I like the sound of this Walter guy."

Tiny Lanirche: "You would. He sounds old and foolish to me. Just spouting off what he thought a young kid like you wanted to hear."

Going crazy Joshua: "Perhaps, but man, did he seem different. He was just so cool. And his wife didn't have crazy purple hair or anything like that, so that's a plus."

Tiny Apostolos: "Walter was right, Joshua. It isn't too late for you. You can still return to the proper path."

Tiny Lanirche: "He *is* on the proper path. Just keep going, Joshua. Besides, you can't go back through that big door. The only option is to follow my letter and come find me. I'll help you find your way in the world."

Regaining sanity Joshua: "Either way, Lanirche is right. I tried that big door, and there is no way I can get back through it alone. I have to find some answers before I can even think about getting back on the narrow path."

Tiny Apostolos: "But Joshua —"

Joshua caught himself and shook his head. There was something in the air here that was making him go crazy. He was starting to hallucinate, and he knew if he didn't find help soon, he would eventually start talking to himself exclusively. The time for thinking was over, it was now time for action.

Joshua peered out into the darkness of the city called Lovelight. A heavy mist was being carried through the streets, and at times it seemed to even have a life of its own as it twirled and tumbled across the asphalt sidewalks. For a city with light in its name, Joshua thought this place was creepily dark. He could barely see anything. He could scarcely make out a few buildings up ahead, and also what looked like neon lights, but that was it. He did, however, see a street lamp nearby that had just flicked to life and decided it would be best to head towards it to get a better view.

As he drew closer, he started to notice this wasn't so much a street lamp as it was a torch. It all seemed pretty medieval to Joshua, but who was he to say anything? This whole experience felt like a weird dream, after all. And who was to say it wasn't all just that? One big weird dream from which he would soon wake up. One can hope, I guess.

Joshua reached the first torch post and began to look around the city of Lovelight. He saw what he assumed was a bar a few blocks down with a flashing sign that read, "Woeful Discourse."

This was the only sign that he could read in the dark, but he could also make out a few more neons further down the block.

He was standing on what appeared to be Lovelight's main street. He saw multiple side streets, but they all branched off this main path. At the far end of the main street he could see a giant skyscraper that seemed to spiral forever into the clouds. Plastered on the side of the building was a giant neon sign that read, "Lanirche, Inc."

"All roads lead to Rome," he thought to himself.

Looking around, Joshua thought the bar would be the best place to obtain information (and maybe some Irish courage) and headed off in that direction. He was startled by an odd popping noise. He jerked his head around and looked for the source of the sound, but saw nothing.

"Hel … help … me."

Joshua, once again startled (and frightened this time), looked in all directions for the voice.

"Please … just a drop … help … just a drop."

He heard the voice stronger this time, and followed it until his eyes were drawn up to the top of the torch post. What he saw made his insides turn to pudding. Joshua wanted to vomit but couldn't. Looking down upon him was a body set afire. The man looked down at Joshua, and in his eyes was a sadness that nobody in the world could ever imagine or comprehend.

"My tongue … just a drop … help … tell my fam … tell my …"

Joshua watched in horror as the man slowly burned to death. He stood until nothing was left but hanging bones. The last remaining ember died out, and Joshua, in disbelief, watched it smolder its last. The ashes from the ground began to rise, floating up through the air, as they reformed themselves on the skeleton hanging from the pole. Joshua watched as organs began to rebuild. He watched as muscle and skin regenerated as if magnetized to the man's skeleton. Within seconds, the man's face had assembled itself again. His eyelids jolted open, and he stared at Joshua with that same sadness. The man shrieked in pain as flames burst forth once more and engulfed his body.

"Have you ... no ... sir ... tell them all ... tell ... just a drop."

The human torch whimpered, as the process repeated itself all over again. Joshua tried to reach up to loosen the man, to cut the ropes that bound him to the pole. The flames were far too intense, though, and he knew that nothing could be done to help him. Joshua turned his face away and began to cry. His tears evaporated as soon as they left his eyes. There would be no water of any kind in this barren place.

Joshua headed off to the neon lights of the bar as he saw hundreds of more torches flare up and die out all along the main street. He imagined thousands, no, millions of torches like this around the city—not torches—people he reminded himself. He had to talk to someone, he had to get answers, and above all, he had to get out of this accursed place.

As he reached the door of the bar, he took a deep breath and wondered what that sign had said on the gate into Lovelight.

It wouldn't be until later that he would find out its true meaning, but the people of the town knew it all too well. The sign on the door read something like this, "Abandon all hope ye' who enter here." He opened the door to the bar of Woeful Discourse and stepped through the archway. Ironically enough, there would be someone inside who knew his name.

11

A Dead Guy Walks Into A Bar ...

OST BARS IN JOSHUA'S WORLD HAD NAMES that brought about a sense of happiness or seemed to say, "Hey, come on in. Good times will be had here!" But with a name like "Woeful Discourse," Joshua didn't know what to expect. The door swung open and Joshua was surprised to see what appeared to be a normal bar. There were the classic hanging green stained glass lights, your basic pool tables, neon signs that advertised various beers and even a genuine looking bar. The bar was also packed with people, who, oddly enough, all looked fairly normal.

The jukebox was playing what Joshua thought was "Hotel California," but he couldn't be sure. It skipped constantly and was hard to make out. CD's probably don't have a great shelf like in a place like this. There was even a classic scruffy, scary bartender behind the counter. The one thing he didn't notice, however, as he walked towards the bar, was Skinless sitting in one of the back booths.

As Joshua sat down at the counter, he could feel the people in the room staring at him. He looked at the bartender now walking towards him from behind the counter, and felt a lump rising in his throat. The bartender's face was beyond scarred and every once in a while, he would wince as if he was in some sort of fantastic pain. He met the bartender's eyes and felt that same sadness that he saw in the human torch outside. He also saw a hatred in his eyes; an abhorring.

"Well, well, Skinless has been neglecting his duties I see." The bartender was right in front of Joshua now, and he smelt of body odor and garbage.

"My name's Joshua. I guess you could say I'm new to the area." Joshua meant this to be an icebreaker–almost a joke–but the bartender just stared at him, still wincing in pain every few seconds. An awkward silence fell over the bar. Joshua sat nervously waiting for the bartender to respond. Begging for him to speak, wink, breathe, laugh, fart–do anything. Just as the silence was about to become unbearable, it was finally broken as the song on the jukebox changed to what now sounded like "The Devil Went Down to Georgia". The bartender dropped his gaze from Joshua and started to convulse. Joshua wondered if he should help. He reached his hand out across the bar, his chain dragging across the counter-top. As quick as lightning, the bartender grabbed Joshua's hand and slammed it down on the counter.

"Keep down, boy. Stay quiet. Do you know where you are right now? Are you so foolish that you would come to Lovelight when you have been given freedom?" The bartender, still squeezing Joshua's arm tightly, loosened his grip.

"These chains around your wrists. I know these all too well," the bartender said, examining them.

"I have never noticed these chains before, and I can only think that they were put on me when I entered this land," Joshua said slightly offended. "Do you know of a way that I may be rid of them?"

"I think you already know that yourself. I think you also know that this place is not the place to be rid of anything. As far as not noticing them, I find that hard to believe. Most people who come to Lovelight flaunted their chains in the other world. They wore them as a badge of honor, and followed their markings to the letter. Here, look." The bartender lifted one of Joshua's chains and revealed the markings that surrounded the outside of the metal. Joshua saw a strange writing that he could not understand.

"But I can't read what it says," exclaimed Joshua, who was now very puzzled.

"Are you so sure? Look closer." The bartender rubbed the inscription, and as he did the metal chipped away. Underneath was clearly written the word, "Pride." He did this with three other chains as well. The words "Lust", "Envy", and "Greed", could clearly be read.

"Enough!" Joshua whispered contritely, as he pulled the chains out of the bartender's hands. "I have seen enough. I get it." The bartender gave a soft smile, somewhat delighting in Joshua's painful realization.

"I need information. Can you help me or not?" Joshua said indignantly, having felt very wronged by the bartender's examination.

"I can help you, yes. But *will* I help you is another matter entirely," the bartender scoffed.

"Well, will you help me then?" Joshua said sarcastically.

"I will help you. Not out of generosity, for that sort of thing will never be found here, but out of pity. I pity you because you have before you an opportunity. Something that I once had but wasted." The bartender looked especially sad after saying this. The man's face changed, and behind those scars, Joshua could see what used to be a handsome man. That was, of course, before he had entered this city.

"Ask your questions, but make it quick. Lanirche's eyes are everywhere in Lovelight."

"Okay, first off then who is Lanirche and why is he after me? Does this Skinless guy work for him or what?" Joshua asked, observing the way the bartender had twitched at the mention of both Lanirche and Skinless.

"Lanirche is, how did we used to say it in your world? I guess he is the … mayor, yeah, that's it. He is the mayor of Lovelight, but he is so much more than that. We had a name for him in your world, but he hates that title and has restricted us from ever calling him that here. As for Skinless, he is his right hand man. Every hundred years or so Lanirche finds a new one. Skinless is his latest model. And I guess your last question was …"

"I want to know why they are after me. Why was I locked up?" Joshua asked again, frustrated at having to repeat his question.

"Ahh yes, that's an easy one. You see, they own you. You escaped. I assume not on your own accord though, yes? Probably one of the Prophet's men? The Prophet is sort of like, what's the word? I guess you would call Him the President of this world. Lanirche is limited in power, and whenever the Prophet takes one of his disciples, he is none too pleased. Most recently, Lanirche had attempted to assassinate the Prophet, but news is, the Prophet lives. That, coupled with your escape … I am sure you can imagine his frustration at the moment."

The bartender winced once more, catching a glass in midair that he had dropped from the pain.

"But they don't own me. Nobody owns me. I am my own person, I own myself. I make my own decisions," Joshua said.

"And how has making your own decisions worked out for you thus far?" the bartender laughed. "Either way you spin it kid, what I said was true."

"Well, let me ask you another question. What's up with this bar? Better yet, what, or where, is Lovelight?" At this, the bartender laughed once more. His jovial attitude did not last long, however, for he was soon brought back into that deep odd pain and was somber once again.

"Listen kid," he said, "this here may look like a bar, but it's actually the middle ring. Lovelight is filled with places just like this. Depending on how you lived your life and what your various 'passions' were, you get divided up to different departments, so to speak. In life I was an alcoholic who murdered my wife and children, and then I killed myself. I woke up here, and have been here ever since. I am told in a couple of years I will be brought to the Abyss. There I will be in a, well, let's just say it's a 'thorny' situation," he continued.

"Everyone in here has a similar story. We sit here and remember the pain we have caused. Waiting and watching as more come, and more leave. Those who leave head to the Abyss never to be seen again. We stay here for all eternity, taunted by the alcohol always around us, but we're never allowed to drink any. I'm here, and I mourn my life. I mourn for everyone in here and for the lives of my family. I am sorry if that is more than what you asked, but I needed to get that off my chest."

The man ached with discomfort, and Joshua reached out to grab his hand to console him. In doing so, his mind clouded just as it had with Apostolos earlier. Joshua's eyes went white, and in his mind a scene played out.

He is in a dark room, and unable to move. He watches as the bartender stumbles into his house with a shotgun in his hands. He sees him kick open a door and shoot his wife, watches as he throws his seven year old daughter off his arm and reloads. The man aims at the little girl, puts his finger on the trigger and ...Joshua pulled his arm away as the man flinched. He had seen enough. The bartender gripped the counter for a moment and continued.

"We stay in a constant state of woeful discourse with each other, and every few seconds, we get flashes of the people we killed or hurt in our lives due to our own selfishness. I hear their cries, I see my wife's face as I put the gun to her head and pull the trigger. I want to cry as I relive the moment where I hold my dead daughter in my arms, but I can't. I can't cry! That is why I cringe in pain, because each time I see it, I feel their pain in the flesh. I have felt it for forty-three years and will continue to feel it for all eternity. As for this place, Lovelight, you're at the gateway to Hell."

Joshua sat in disbelief and listened as the bartender explained these things. He sat and thought only of how much he wanted to get up and leave immediately, but he couldn't. He felt as if he were glued to his seat; as if some unknown force wanted him to hear it all.

"I hate you, and yet I would never wish this upon you. That is why I have answered your questions. You must avoid Skinless and Lanirche at all costs. Skinless' old master was Death, but Death has recently gone missing. The one whom Death served, however, is the master of all. He is the prince of the air. He is the one you must be wary of, for he will trick and deceive you. He is the father of lies. He is of course, the one and only, Lanirche."

The bartender stumbled backwards, crashing into the shelf behind him. Bottles came tumbling down to the ground, stopping just short and hovering inches from the floor. The shelf popped back into its bracket on the wall, as the bottles floated back to their resting places. The bar went silent for what seemed like a minute. A short stumpy man in the back corner let out a shrill scream, finally breaking the silence. The man's scream was like a contagious yawn, and soon the entire bar was back to its wailing and moaning.

The bartender seemed to be in astronomical pain after having mentioned Lanirche's name. He recovered himself and continued, this time leaning in even closer. Smelling the man's breath was like inhaling deeply into a trashcan, but Joshua kept himself composed.

"Only one has ever come back from the Abyss," the bartender whispered. "Only one has ever escaped the master's grasp. He is the one we call The Prophet. I wish I could remember His name. He is the only one that Lanirche fears. He alone can help you. You must find Him before Lanirche finds you. Other than what I have told you, I can't do anything else for ya. I will most likely be sent to the Abyss ahead of schedule for what little I have told you already," the bartender sighed to himself. Longing for a second chance at life. "My name is Pierre. Don't forget my story ... umm?"

"Joshua. My name is Joshua."

"Always remember what you have seen here Joshua. Now leave before your–"

The bartender's eyes lit up with fear as he spied the man sitting in the back booth who was now getting up. The bartender's mouth fell open, as he cowered beneath the counter. Joshua turned around, spying that familiar hooded figure in the back corner of the bar. As Skinless made his way towards Joshua, a man from a nearby booth fell to the floor blocking his path. The man writhed on the ground, pulling his hair out as he wailed. Skinless gave a sharp kick, sending the man gliding across the floor. Joshua took this opportunity to run. He leapt off the bar stool and rushed for the door. All the while, Skinless watched, and somewhere beneath that hood, he smiled.

12
IN THE SHADOW OF WINGS

J OSHUA GRABBED THE DOOR and threw it open. He rushed out into the darkness, and the screaming behind him lessened as the door closed shut. He wondered what the man in the bar who had screamed must have seen in his head that would have made him tear his own hair out. If it was anything like what he had witnessed in the bartender's head, he could only imagine; he probably didn't want to know.

He looked back and saw the door fly open once more. Skinless came rushing out and was yelling in some foreign language. Joshua darted for one of the side streets, as the sound of sirens echoed throughout the city. He found himself staring into a massive hole in the ground. If his senses hadn't been so heightened from the rush of adrenaline, he may have fallen into the hole and ended all this madness right then. That hole was probably what Lanirche called the "scenic route" to the Abyss. He heard screams coming from deep within, and could feel intense heat gushing out from the gaping hole. The smell of sulfur was pungent in the air, and it burned his nostrils as he caught his breath.

He rushed back onto the main street and burst into a full on sprint. Glancing behind, he could clearly see Skinless moving at a remarkable speed (for a man with almost no muscle to speak of) as he chased him. With each step Skinless took, he gained a little more ground. His steps sounded like bamboo shoots smacking cement, as the pure bone of Skinless' feet hit the pavement hard. Joshua turned his head, focused on his path, and rushed down another side street. Looking back once more, he saw not only

Skinless, but many others turning the corner in pursuit of him. He ran even faster now—adrenaline coursing through his body and keeping his feet quick.

Joshua could see the human torches slowly dropping from their posts and joining Skinless in hot pursuit. To him, they looked like ambulance lights, flashing red and yellow as the flames flicked off their bodies as they ran. Joshua was stopped in his tracks as one of them dropped right in front of him. The sheer heat coming off the human torch was so hot that it burnt the hairs off his right arm as he swatted the monster away. He tried running down yet another street but was blocked by another hole.

In this hole, he thought he saw a giant serpent moving far below; a serpent that was hundreds of miles long. High above him he could hear the flapping of wings. Looking up into the misty night air, he could see a creature with three faces circling overhead. One face was human, one beast, and one reptilian.

He was trapped it seemed, and this was it. He would be captured and sent to the Abyss for eternity. Skinless probably had something special cooked up for him this time, as well, for escaping.

Joshua was surrounded from all sides, flaming corpses on the left, Skinless and a small army of the damned to his right, a giant hole with a huge serpent to his back, not to mention the creature above. Joshua closed his eyes and waited. As he closed his eyes he whispered.

"Apostolos, I am sorry, friend. Please, please help me once more. I can't do this without you ... without your Master."

Joshua waited for the hands of the damned to seize him, but he waited in vain. Behind his closed eyes, a light began to shine. He opened his eyelids and saw his would-be kidnappers frozen in fear. Standing before them was a man with a face that shone like the sun. The man turned and faced Joshua. Joshua lowered his eyes, and falling to his knees, spoke.

"Are you with me, or with my enemies?" Joshua asked the radiant being in front of him as all those around him stood catatonic in their places.

"No," he replied, "but as one of the generals of the army of the Lord, I have now come."

The man carried an orange sword with the symbol of a snake wrapped around a staff on it. With each word from the man's lips, a shockwave of ghastly beautiful light emanated from his body.

"Please help me. Save me from these creatures who mean to harm me, from my mortal enemies who have surrounded me," Joshua said, feeling as if something inside him was speaking for him, mediating this whole transaction.

"Hide me in the shadow of your wings," he added. These last words rolled out of Joshua's mouth and he knew not what they meant.

The man looked down at Joshua and said, "Take heart. I serve the one true King, and not even the mighty gates of Pandemonium can withstand Him." The man turned around, his back now facing Joshua. "Put your back to mine, and quick!" the shining man said. Joshua spun around and backed up into the shining man who now had his sword drawn and was slashing it at the creatures surrounding them. Two of the man's four large wings surrounded Joshua turning him into a sort of human backpack.

Joshua felt himself being lifted as the shining man stretched out his two remaining wings and beat down hard against the air. Skinless screamed out a command to the creature flying above to attack. Peering through the wings of his transport, Joshua saw the winged beast come swooping in with claws outstretched. The shining man lifted his sword which ignited with blue fire, and swung at the beast. The creature dodged, diving in and using its lion like claws to cut a gash into one of the shining man's four wings. The two wings carrying Joshua loosened, and Joshua went falling back towards the hellish ground.

The shining man pulled the injured wing behind him and dove headfirst for Joshua's free-falling, flailing body. The creature, which was now right on the shining man's heels, also dove for Joshua but with its claws outstretched.

"Behind you!" Joshua screamed as he fell. The shining man whipped around faster than lightning and dug his flaming sword into the belly of the beast. The creature let out a horrendous shriek and fled as blood gushed forth onto the heads of Skinless and his posse below. Joshua turned midair and saw that he was just seconds from hitting pavement. His eyes went black as he passed out from the shock. The shining man dove with all his speed, taking hold of Joshua's limp body just before it hit the ground. Joshua's chains sparked as they dragged along the pavement, and the shining man beat his wings hard to quickly gain height.

A few of the human torches jumped at the shining man, his feathers scorching as their fiery hands grasped for his wings. Skinless was screaming out commands this entire time, as the monsters on the ground crawled over one another making a mountain of bodies. There were thousands of creatures now running the streets of Lovelight, and the shining man was doing the best he could to avoid the flesh mountains.

Skinless knew that the winged man would have to head to the main gate in order to leave the city. He would have to act fast if he was going to stop Joshua from escaping again. Skinless knelt down, scratching a symbol into the main streets pavement. He pulled back, and the pavement began to glow bright red. The cement under the symbol began to melt, and many of the creatures pursuing the shining man fell into the hot magma that lay below the chasm.

A loud guttural roar pierced the night air, and Cerberus, "The three-headed Hellhound," emerged from the molten lava. Shaking the lava off like a dog would shake water, the beast came sprawling forth and heeled before Skinless who in turn jumped on his back.

"After them!" Skinless yelled, as he kicked the great beast's sides. Cerberus galloped after the flying man down the main street. Joshua opened his blurry eyes. Head pounding from all the noise, he took one look at the fiery hell hound with Skinless screaming curses on his back, and immediately passed out once more. The great Cerberus vaulted over a wave of human torches, and clung to the side of a building digging his claws into the metal framework. Running alongside the walls of the skyscrapers, Skinless tried his best to hold on, kicking the beast harder.

"Back on the ground you fool! Get back on the ground!"

Cerberus, ignoring the kicks and groans of his rider, dug his claws in harder and climbed even higher along the side of the building.

The shining man was only a hundred feet or so from the main gate, when out of the darkness the great beast came hurtling through the night air. Having only had seconds to react, he swooped low and dropped Joshua's unconscious body right in front of the colossal doors just before getting caught in the arms of the massive beast. The shining man went tumbling forth on the hard ground as the beast landed and circled round.

"It's over Metatron!" Skinless barked. "That boy belongs to Lanirche. Your Master has meddled in our affairs for far too long!"

Skinless dismounted the great creature, approaching Joshua as the legions of the damned flooded the main street in front of them. The shining man rose to his feet spitting blood from his mouth.

"You think this boy belongs to Lanirche?" Metatron laughed. "My Master seems to think otherwise. And, as you know, He is never wrong." Metatron walked over to Joshua's side and picked the boy up with ease, throwing him over his shoulder. The winged man limped towards the towering door, turning his back to Skinless and the army of the damned.

"You think we are just going to let you walk out of here Metatron?" Skinless howled.

"Who said I needed your permission?" the shining man said looking over the shoulder opposite of his cargo. The winged man placed both his hands (one on each side) of the doors and pushed. The magnificent gate creaked open. Standing on the other side of the gate were thousands of winged men and women all just like Metatron, and all armed to the teeth. They were shining so brightly that it looked as if the sun were biased to this side of the gate.

"Remember, Skinless," Metatron said, "It is you and Lanirche that have to ask permission of *our* Master." The shining man advanced through the gates with Joshua still bent over his shoulder. Skinless thought for a second, and then waved his arm forward for his army to march into battle, but nobody dared budge. Cerberus went whimpering back into his lava hole, and the army dispersed as the colossal gates of Lovelight closed behind Metatron.

Skinless cursed into the hot night air. He could almost see Mr. Vlad's smile in the back of his mind. He would certainly be paying him another visit very soon.

13

THE ANGEL IN THE AMBULANCE

N AMBULANCE, back on the busy streets of Chicago ...

"Anyways, I told Charlie that if he keeps pushing my buttons like he has been it's lights out for that joker."

Luke listened to his "friend" Wilson ramble on as usual. He didn't mind it so much though; the more Wilson talked, the less he had to, and that was a good thing in his eyes. Luke had always been the quiet type; in high school, college, and eventually even in medical school. Most of the other people he graduated with went on to be plastic surgeons or work in fancy ER's all over the world, but Luke just wanted to be an EMT. The way he saw it, he could save more lives by getting to the person at the scene of the accident, rather than getting to them ten minutes too late in the ER.

Every once in a while, he would run into one of his old classmates from school.

"What are you up to nowadays, Luke?" they would ask knowing full well "what he was up to." Luke would just smile at them and with a big grin say, "just doing the Lord's work." He never stayed around to explain what he meant, just seeing the reaction of his classmate was good enough for him. He would shake their hands, and then rush off to find the nearest bathroom to wash the filthy smell of money off his. To Luke, all their hands smelt like money, and no matter how hard they washed, it always sweated through; it was in their blood.

"Are you listening to me at all, Luke?" Wilson asked.

"Yeah man, sorry. You know me, I space out sometimes," Luke replied.

"Well anyways, like I was saying. That dog has been biting my hand for over three years now and if he—"

The radio beeps and stops Wilson mid-sentence. A woman's voice is heard and both men in the ambulance go silent.

"We have a Code 14, shots fired in alleyway of Judge's Suites at the corner of 1st and Nun. Police have been alerted."

"Rock and roll, baby!"

Wilson slams his foot on the gas, as Luke rolls his eyes. Two minutes after the call the two men come driving in sirens blaring. They manage to beat the cops, and already a crowd is forming. The two men jump out of the ambulance while Wilson runs around the back to grab the gurney. Luke grabs his orange "bag o' healing" (as Wilson calls it), and pushes through the spectators.

Three bodies lay before him and he immediately starts checking their vitals. One dead, one with a weak pulse, and one who should recover. The world around him moves in slow motion as he works his hands like an artist before a canvas. This is what he was born to do, this is his calling. Police sirens start to blare as squad cars and other ambulances pull up. Luke tunes out the noise and hears only silence. He is painting a tapestry and must not be disturbed. Bandage here, snip there, hook up to fluids, strap on gurney, back of the ambulance, and before the crowd even knows what just happened, both of the men are back in the ambulance and on their way to the hospital.

Luke stays in the back and tends to his masterpiece, as Wilson makes the road his canvas and paints some beautiful strokes up Fifth Avenue. Luke grabs the radio and starts making his report as feverishly and efficiently as possible.

"This is unit seven reporting a Code 14. Hospital destination is Willow Creek, ETA is …" Luke looks up at Wilson who shoots up four fingers in the air.

"ETA is four minutes. We have one male in critical condition. Three bodies in all at the scene, one of the other two was DOA, while the other was in stable condition. Multiple gunshot wounds on all three bodies."

"Thank you unit seven, we will see you shortly," the woman's voice answers.

Luke looks down at the young man strapped before him. The boy's eyes open slightly and meet Luke's.

"Hey big guy. You are hurt pretty bad, but we got you now. Can you tell me your name?" Luke asks.

"Are you with me …?" The young man creaks the words out of his mouth. "Hide me … in your wing …" The young man closes his eyes once more and is silent.

Luke checks the man's pockets, and pulls out a wallet. Checking his license, he reads the name: Joshua Hawkins. Grabbing the radio, Luke relays the boy's info to the dispatcher.

He has heard the name before. "Hawkins," he thinks to himself. "Could his brother be …?" The chances are one in a million probably, but still, if it was his brother …

"Step on it Wilson. I can't lose this one." Luke yells through the tiny window into the driver's seat.

The four minutes tick by in a flash and they arrive at Willow Creek Hospital. As the hospital personnel pull the bodies out from the back of the ambulances, Luke catches glimpses of all three of the bodies. The man that didn't make it has a face that is old and tired but peaceful. The second is twitching slightly and in a lot of pain. Lastly, (his masterpiece) the third is young and rugged, not much unlike himself.

Luke and his partner hop back in the ambulance after filling out reports, and head back to clean up and end their shift.

"Those guys were in really bad shape Luke, but I got to tell you man, the way you work is a heck of a thing to watch. If it had been anyone else with me today that guy wouldn't even have a chance right now; it's a thing of beauty you do out there."

Luke turns and smiles, "Just doing the Lord's work, my friend. Just doing the Lord's work."

PART TWO:

STUMBLE

1

ON THE ROAD AGAIN

JOSHUA AWOKE IN BRIGHT LIGHT. He had an aching back and a stiff neck, a few cuts and bruises as well, but other than that, he seemed fine. The back of his head throbbed just as it had before, in the cell, but soon the ache went away after a bit of rubbing. He examined his surroundings and found that he was no longer in Lovelight but back once more at the crossroads. In fact, he knew in some strange way that he was laying exactly where his prison cell had once been. He sat up, rubbed the sleep out of his eyes, and had no sooner returned to his feet before he heard a familiar voice.

"Hello Joshua," the voice said. "I have returned to set you on the right path once more."

Sitting before him, in what looked like a lawn chair, was his guide, his friend, his brother; Apostolos.

"Apostolos," Joshua started, "I'm sorry, I don't know what to say. I should have followed your advice. I should have listened to your words. Tell me more of your Master! Tell me what I must do to be saved and be rid of these accursed chains!"

"No need now, Joshua," replied Apostolos. "My King knows what is in a man. You must follow the path that He has laid out for you, for it will lead you to His kingdom and to everlasting life. It will not be an easy one, but my Master will refine you into the man that He knows you can be, who He made you to be. I must leave you, but know that you are never alone for He has placed His Spirit upon you Joshua, and none can pluck you from His hand."

Apostolos began to rise from his chair but sat back down seeing that Joshua still had many questions.

"Apostolos, I'm scared, where are you going? Where is the winged man who saved me? Why can't you come with me?" Joshua asked, still looking up at Apostolos like a long lost family member reunited.

"I must go ahead," Apostolos replied, "for there is much work to be done. The man who saved you was one of the leaders in the Master's army. He aided you because you asked for my Master's help. But now is not the time for talking, but for action. Lanirche thought that he had destroyed our King for good. He may be the father of lies, but he is also the father of fools! My Master has risen, and there is much work to be done. I will go ahead of you, Joshua, and meet you just outside of the woods. There you will be set free of your chains, for it is the hill outside of those woods where my Master defeated Death, himself! Now go Joshua and follow the path set before you."

"But how will I know the path through the woods? How can I know the way?" Joshua asked.

Apostolos smiled getting up from his chair.

"My Master is the Way, Joshua. Follow the narrow path, friend. Do not be afraid. It is we who should be feared." And with that, Apostolos was gone in a flash of light.

Joshua sat in the open field with tears in his eyes. His heart felt whole for once in his life. He didn't want a drink, he didn't want women or drugs, he didn't want to have fortune or fame. All he wanted was to see the King's face and to thank Him. He knew at that moment that he loved Him, he wasn't sure why just yet or how, but he loved Him.

Joshua got to his feet and brushed the grass and dirt off of his jeans. As he did so, he felt something in his back pocket. He pulled it out and was surprised to find the letter that Lanirche had left him when he first escaped his prison cell. He pulled it out and read once more, except this time the words were different.

Joshua Hawkins,

You caused quite a stir in Lovelight my friend (not to mention tons of property damage), but I am incredibly forgiving, you see. I could see how you would think ill of me, what with Skinless and his shenanigans. I assure you; I had nothing to do with his antics. Skinless is what we in the biz call a "loose cannon." I can tell you with full confidence, that all responsible in the Lovelight incident have been severely reprimanded. I actually encourage you to take the path into the woods this time and wish you the best. Looking forward to seeing you face-to-face very soon!

Your friend,
Lanarche

Joshua crumpled up the piece of paper and threw it on the ground. He felt a slight jostle in his back pocket, and reaching back once more, pulled out the same letter. This process was repeated at least ten or twenty times, each time lending the same results. Sighing, Joshua was content to just ignore the piece of paper for now. Something he couldn't ignore, however, was the last line.

"Looking forward to seeing you face-to-face very soon!" Joshua did not share the same sentiments, however.

Joshua was at a crossroad in his life, but this time, his heart was light and he knew the path he should take. He was ready to be rid of these blasted chains, which, coincidentally grew heavier after having left Lovelight. He stepped onto the narrow path that led into the dark forest. The trees seemed alive, and Joshua felt as if millions of eyes were watching his every movement. This path that lay before him would most certainly not be easy. To say that Joshua was scared would have been an understatement. Apostolos' song came to his mind, and in a way, it helped to alleviate some of his fears. He repeated it to himself out loud as he entered the forest.

"It was a strange and dreadful strife
when life and death contended;
The victory remained with life;
the reign of death was ended.
Stripped of power, no more it reigns,
an empty form alone remains
Death's sting is lost forever! Alleluia!"

Alleluia, he thought, alleluia ...

2
The Ghost Tree's Song

 BAR IN CHICAGO, three years ago ...

A man sits in a corner of a bar in Chicago and tells a story about a tree. The men and women around him listen on hoping to get a good laugh.

"Stupid old drunk!" one yells; "lazy fool!" yet another screams. The leader of their pack pours his beverage all over the man and the crowd gets one final laugh before returning to their seats. The old man sits drenched in the corner licking his lips, taking in every drop that finds its way to his mouth, and as he does a song leaves his furled lips in a whisper.

Hear; oh hear the Ghost Tree's song,
Its not quite short, but it isn't long,
It looms in the forest black as night,
Anxious and waiting to snuff out the light.

The Devil himself planted the seed,
At the dawn of time, he set it free,
Watered with tears and fed with flesh,
It devours bones and creates unrest.

Lovers that come and bask in its shade,
Soon find love lost, no hearts carved today,
Their minds grow apart, and are soon far away,
For trusting the Ghost Tree, the lovers part ways.

Many have tried to cut down this tree,
Some who come close lose their sanity,
Their story is heard in bars all around,
Of how the Ghost Tree, almost came down.

Those who walk past feel tired and cold,
They come very young, and leave very old,
The tree casts a spell which few can resist,
It lures in the weak with the promise of bliss.

Hear; oh hear the Ghost Tree's song,
It wasn't quite short, but it didn't last long,
It waits in the forest black as night,
Laughing and grinning as it snuffs out the light.

The old man finishes his song and takes one last look at the boy who has drenched him with beer. He looks at Joshua's laughing face and stumbles out of the bar.

3
FOREST OF ABSALOM

J•OSHUA WALKED FOR A WHILE on the narrow cobblestone path that led deeper into the forest. With each step, the forest grew darker and more overgrown. The sound of wild animals could be heard, and Joshua was constantly checking his back to make sure he wasn't being followed. He also heard the sound of many voices whispering all around him. He could swear that he heard his name being called every so often, but told himself it was only the wind and nothing more. Venturing further, he came across a sign buried in the ground that read:

FOREST OF ABSALOM
BEWARE THE GHOST TREE

"Ghost Tree?" Joshua spoke quietly ...

He thought that he had heard this name before—perhaps in a bar? He remembered vaguely an old drunk talking about a grand camping trip that he once took when he came upon a giant tree in the forest. The tree, he said, sang to him; said it held him in its branches and lulled him to sleep. If it hadn't been for his wife calling behind him, he said he probably would have stayed there for the rest of his life.

"Ghost Tree," the old man said, "Avoid the Ghost Tree!"

"Just the ramblings of a loony old drunk." Joshua had thought at the time, but now; now he wasn't sure what to make of it.

He stepped onto the leafy path and noticed that the narrow cobblestone road had ended and was replaced by an even tighter path leading deeper into the woods. In some areas he would have to turn sideways to squeeze through the underbrush. The road was now about the size of a bike path he guessed. "Did they even have bikes here?" he wondered. Every now and then, a rogue branch would appear out of nowhere and cut into Joshua's face or clothesline him, sending him sprawling to the forest floor. The leaves would rustle all about him, making it sound as if the forest itself was laughing. The chains around Joshua's ankles and wrists seemed to be growing heavier with each step as well, and they kept catching onto roots and branches as he delved deeper into the Forest of Absalom.

He had finally realized the full extent of the burden which he bore, and was ready to be freed from these chains forever. Joshua tripped over a maverick root, and a rock from the path cut straight through his jeans and into his knee. Blood trickled down his leg, but the pain was bearable for now.

Joshua's clothes were now seeped in sweat, and as he went further in, the trees grew larger and thicker, blocking out the light coming from the sky. The whispering voices were also growing louder now as he plunged deeper into the bowels of the forest. An occasional cobweb would smack his face, and he would go into a crazy swiping mode as most sane people do in similar situations.

Joshua ducked his head to avoid being clotheslined on another hanging branch, and as he did, he noticed a large pile of rocks just off the main path. He would have gone to have a look, had he not heard a loud hissing noise right below his feet. He kicked his legs frantically, and started into a full on run down the narrow path. A large limb whacked into his right eye causing it to water and blur. He slowed his pace and let it water until he regained vision. He began to think about the shining man and Pierre in the bar. He also began to wonder what was happening to his real body in his world. His original thoughts of death came flooding back into his mind. Was this purgatory? Was he dead? All the while, the thought of the Ghost Tree seemed to slip his mind more and more as the forest grew darker and darker.

4
STRAYING FROM THE PATH

HOURS PASSED AS JOSHUA TRUDGED on and on through the forest of Absalom. He was tired, hungry, and now very thirsty. He had been walking for hours and was relieved at the sound of running water. It turned out to only be a tiny creek, but water was water, and he drank heavily until he could hear it sloshing around inside his belly. He also found some berries that looked edible and he began to gorge himself on them until he was full.

Joshua pressed on yet deeper into the forest. He came across what looked like a makeshift campsite, but the wood for the fire looked very old and the ground around it was now thickly covered with leaves. Perhaps if he had come back through this part of the woods fifty years ago, he would have found travelers just like himself sitting around a fire swapping stories or songs.

The sound of wildlife and whispering had been pretty prevalent up until this point and the silence made Joshua uneasy. He pressed on thinking about Apostolos and his Master. He had known of Him in his life but always thought his teachings were a bunch of hogwash, no better than voodoo, as it were. He still didn't understand the whole cannibal sacrament thing, where Christians ate the Jesus guy's flesh or whatever. He would have to ask Apostolos about that one. He almost thought it comical that it took him dying to discover the way to live; or perhaps he always knew deep down inside.

Sweat dropped into Joshua's eyes and he wiped it off. As the salt stung his pupils, he rubbed his eyelids and started seeing those weird little floating lights. He remembered his father telling him when he was little that they were tiny boats that sailed through the watery parts of your eye.

"The lights are lanterns that are fixed to the bow of the fisherman's boats," his father would explain. All very foolish, but a fond memory none the less. As his eyes cleared, he imagined the tiny boats sinking and the captains going down with them into the deep blue depths of his cornea. Though his eyes had cleared, however, he realized that there was still one light floating in the middle of his vision. He kept pushing forward through the thick brush and noticed it was getting closer. This wasn't a trick of the eyes, but instead, he knew it was an exit he was seeing.

Excited by the light at the end of the tunnel, he rushed on as fast as his throbbing knee would allow. It was still bleeding from the nasty cut he had received earlier, and now that his blood was pumping harder, he could feel it beating intensely. The light grew closer, and as it did, Joshua grew more and more tired. It made him think of how you could say, "okay, three miles and then I'm done running." Somehow, that last mile was always the hardest. But, if you had said to yourself, "okay, five miles and then I'm done," still it would be that fifth mile that gave you the most difficulty. The human mind has a way of tricking you just as you are closest to that which you desire. Joshua even tried telling himself that he didn't care about the light so much, but getting outside of the light. Maybe that would help to trick his mind … it didn't.

Panting now, with a deep pain in his chest and his knee about to give way, Joshua slowed to a crawl. He was so close, but he needed to rest. He came upon a clearing where in the middle sat an enormous tree. A tree that looked so old its seed could have been planted at the beginning of time. There was heavy moss draped on each low hanging branch which made the tree look like an old man with long white hair. The trunk was a shade of dark grey, and the tree looked dry and dead. Perhaps at one point this tree had been young and full of green leaves, but Joshua couldn't picture it. Now it just looked like a ghost of its former self; a Ghost Tree.

As Joshua approached the clearing, he thought of how nice it would be to rest under its shade for a few minutes. And why shouldn't he? He was close yes, but he was tired, and what's a few minutes off the path? He was being drawn to the tree like a magnet. Had he not been in a trance-like state, Joshua would have noticed that the source of the whispers in the forest was rooted right in front of him. In fact, the whispers which had sounded like thousands of different voices at first were now blending and merging into one unified voice. Somewhere, in the back of Joshua's mind he could hear Apostolos' words to stay on the path, but shrugged them off as more of a metaphorical statement than a literal one.

Joshua stepped off the path, and no sooner had his foot touched the ground in the clearing, than he heard a voice call to him.

5
THE ROOTS OF THE WICKED RUN DEEP

"H ELLO, JOSHUA. YOU LOOK TIRED," a voice called from the direction of the clearing, but Joshua could see nobody in sight.

"Who's there? Where are you? I was coming to rest under this tree just for a few minutes but if I am intruding, then I apologize, and I'll be on my way."

"Intruding!? Oh, my dear boy, all are welcome here," the voice spoke, but it sounded as if there were a thousand different voices speaking in unison. "I am a friend, Joshua. Don't be afraid," the voices said. "Come sit under this tree and rest, and I will reveal myself to you. No need to fear, for I am old and could easily be overtaken if I posed any threat to you."

Joshua thought this was probably the truth because the voice which he heard now sounded old and frail. As he inched closer to the tree, he noticed what looked like wooden handles peppered throughout the soil all around the tree. They looked like wooden levers sticking out of the ground, as if you could flip one of them over and it would move the Earth. He moved closer to one on his way to the tree trunk. Walking forward, he realized that they were actually axe handles, though the heads had long since rusted or gone missing. The whole thing was peculiar to say the least, but he was so tired he couldn't think straight long enough to realize that this entire situation felt wrong.

Joshua was only fifty feet away from the tree's enormous trunk when he decided to speak out to the unseen voice. Obviously starting to feel slightly uneasy that somebody, or something, was watching his every move.

"This is close enough, stranger. Now show yourself if you truly are a friend," Joshua said, trying to conceal the fear in his voice.

The tree began to shake in front of Joshua, and the bark itself seemed to crawl over its surface. It moved in patterns and in circles until it formed what looked like eyebrows, then eyes, then a mouth and nose. Joshua was staring into a face, and the tree's eyes opened and stared back.

Joshua, now startled, jumped backwards and tripped over a "conveniently" placed root. Falling to the ground, he began to crab walk backwards with his hands and push with his feet. One of the tree's two enormous branches—which now looked like two powerful arms—swung down and grabbed Joshua around the waist-lifting him up into the air. Screaming as he soared through the air, Joshua was flung upwards and then brought back down to the ground. A massive root began to emerge from the soil and formed a kind of bench for him to sit on. The branch lowered him and sat him down upon the root-bench.

"Calm down, Joshua," the tree said; now choosing the voice of a kind old woman. "You are not the first to have that reaction. Sit and be still while I speak to you." Joshua sat down fearing that, if he ran, another branch would swoop down and swat him like a bug.

"I am the Ghost Tree," the tree continued. "I have been in this world and many others since the beginning of time. My roots run very deep, my little friend. There is not a place on earth where I do not have my ear listening. That is how I know your name. That is how I know you are tired, and that is how I know you are following that fool Apostolos and his crazy teachings."

Joshua flinched at the audacity of the tree to call Apostolos a fool.

"A fool?" Joshua asked. "If you truly knew as much as you say you do then you would know that Apostolos saved me from my prison. He set me free and has placed me on the narrow path. He has told me of his Master and of what I must do to be rid of these blasted chains. Death himself went after the King's Prophet, yet he hasn't returned since, and still you have the gall to call Apostolos foolish? You, Tree, or whatever, are the fool," Joshua finished angrily.

The face of the tree smiled at Joshua and began to chuckle. The laughter of a thousand voices could be heard all around Joshua. It was at this moment, that Joshua realized he was surrounded. The entire forest was all offshoots of this one giant tree. Joshua became filled with rage at the mockery of this creature, but dared not move or say anything knowing that he was powerless in the beast's lair.

"You think you follow the one true King?" the tree boasted, taking a voice with a heavy English accent. "Well let me tell you, human; I saw the one you speak of. I saw him die with my very own eyes, and yes, he was a man. I watched his own people put him on trial and murder him not more than three days ago. Now, your friend Apostolos speaks as if he is still alive? You are more ignorant than you look if you truly believe the Prophet lives."

The Ghost Tree laughed once more. The noise now coming at Joshua in surround sound. He could feel the soil beneath him shaking, as the roots buried deep shook the ground with amusement.

"You saw him die, true, but Apostolos told me He rose from the grave, and even now is with the Master in His kingdom. If you know as much as you say you do, then you would know that He does indeed live."

"I tell you, this man was a fraud and now he rots in the grave where all men eventually go!" The Ghost Tree bellowed loudly, obviously upset at the tone in which Joshua spoke. "No one has ever seen Death and lived. I know this to be a fact. I tell you, your God is dead! You have been deceived by a crazy man's ramblings and now you follow a path that will surely lead you to eternal pain and suffering. Why did Apostolos 'save you', if you are faced with even greater dangers on this narrow path of his? Some savior he was. Why didn't he warn you of Lovelight? Did you really think that would be your only hardship in this harsh land?" The Ghost

Tree now took the voice of a young woman, and brushed his hanging moss back with his branch as if sweeping its hair out of its eyes.

Joshua sat silent, thinking about all that the Ghost Tree had said. Was his mind playing tricks on him, or was this tree lying? "No, he speaks true," he thought. He really saw the Prophet die. Joshua could hear it in his voice … correction, voices. But who sent the Shining Man to save him from Lovelight then? Joshua sat and doubted just like all "wise" men do when faced with the "facts." He was now back in a battle between his heart and his head. His mind told him to listen to the Ghost Tree's words, listen to his reasoning. But deep in his heart, another voice was calling him; a voice that said, "you know the Truth, Joshua. You know Who is the Truth."

"I don't know what to do," Joshua argued. "I'm sitting here talking to a tree. I died for what seems like days ago, and I'm being chased by a skeleton-man and an army of the damned! This is Hell, not Lovelight. The feeling of losing your mind, of having all your truths questioned, that's Hell. I'm going insane, aren't I?"

"Yes, Joshua, you are," the tree answered this time with a voice that sounded like Sigmund Freud's. "You are losing your sanity, because you are dreaming and you cannot make sense of dreams. If you try, you will eventually go insane seeking their meanings. Now, sleep, Joshua. Sleep in my shade, and when you awake, all this will be over, and you will wake up alive and in your bed. Wake up from this dream of following Apostolos and his so called 'king'. Wake up from the lies he supposedly told you, wake up and realize all you need in this world is yourself. The antidote is to get rid of this sentimental religion! Those fools that follow the Prophet make an idol out of fear, and call it God," the tree continued.

"There is no right or wrong path-just the one you make for yourself. Be strong, Joshua. You make your own destiny; you make your own path from now on. If you follow the Prophet's path, you will end up just like Him-dead." The Tree finished, and with his last words Joshua felt a certain recognizable comfort come over him. His chains felt lighter, and the burning red words that had been emblazoned on them began to change once more into that unrecognizable language.

"So this is all just a dream then?" Joshua asked.

"Doesn't it all *feel* like a silly dream, my boy? The master's kingdom and this Lovelight you spoke of. None of that is real. Why, even Skinless and Lanirche are fake. You need not fear such childish beliefs," the tree replied.

The ground began to shake, and springing forth from the soil came a large root that morphed itself into the shape of a bed. The tree shook its limbs hard, and leaves came showering down all around Joshua like a rainstorm of grey dried paper. The root-bed started to fill up with the falling leaves, and had now made a makeshift mattress from them.

"Now, lie down and rest, my child," the tree spoke, this time with the voice of Joshua's mother.

Joshua walked forward, crawled into the root-bed, and sunk deep into the soft dead crackling leaves. He closed his eyes and fell asleep—hoping to wake up from this dream. The Ghost Tree had another victim; another voice to add to his collection, another soul to hand over to Lanirche. Another lost sheep would never be found, and as Joshua lay in the shade of the Ghost Tree, he didn't awake from a dream, but fell into a nightmare.

6
THE SCENE OF THE CRIME

O N A POLICE DESK in Chicago ...

March 16th, 10:13 PM. I responded to a call from an elderly man who reported hearing shots fired in the alleyway of Judge's Suites. Apartment is located on 1st and Nun.

Man sighted perpetrator fleeing down an alleyway after shooting a bystander who confronted him. Another bystander was seen running to the victim's aide and found himself in a fight with the perpetrator. The criminal and bystander wrestled over the gun until shots were fired and both men went down.

When I arrived, the ambulances already had all three bodies and were rushing them off to the ER. I confirmed all this information with the elderly man; Nights, Reuben. He was the one who first made the call. I talked to other witnesses who all said they saw everything but assumed someone else would dial 911. All their stories matched that of Mr. Nights.

Three bodies were found at the scene of the crime. No word yet from the hospital on their conditions, but one of them was confirmed dead at the scene. Presumably it was the young man that first went after the perpetrator. I will file another report once more information is obtained.

I DECLARE, UNDER PENALTY OF PERJURY, THIS STATEMENT OF 1 PAGE IS TRUE AND CORRECT, BASED ON MY PERSONAL KNOWLEDGE.
SIGNATURE OF PERSON GIVING STATEMENT

Louis Hunneh

7

ANOMIE

J•OSHUA WAS WALKING THROUGH SHADES OF GREY. Faces from his past floated by and would evaporate in a whisper as they passed. Their words were jumbled, and he couldn't make out what any of them were saying; just whispers of things forgotten. His great grandfather's face floated past, and Joshua reached out to grab hold of it. The incorporeal image flowed through his fingers like water, and floated away. Many others from his past drifted by, all turning as they did to whisper things into his ear. Joshua's body kept walking though, never allowing him to run after the faces of his past. The face of his brother materialized right in front of him, and he longed to look away but was unable; his body wouldn't allow it. The face was coming right at him. His brother's lips were moving, but Joshua could hear nothing. The face collided into his, and as it did, he heard his brother's voice. "Glamorous, aint it?" the voice said.

Suddenly, the grey colors disappeared, and everything was bright. Joshua found himself walking on what appeared to be the surface of the sun. The flames shot up all around him, but his body just continued to walk. He looked down to see what was holding him up, and found that he appeared to be walking on a giant flaming ball of glass.

He told his legs to stop, and they did. "Bend down," he said, and his body bent down. He pressed his face up against the glass and realized that despite the flames coming off it, it was cool to the touch. He stared into the glass and thought he saw something floating around inside. Once more, as if having to command his body, he called out the word "hit," and his fists began to pound away at the glass.

The glass sphere seemed unfazed at first, and then, the smallest crack began to form. His body–like a remote controlled robot–continued hitting until the crack became a large gash in the sun's exterior.

"Harder," he cried, and his hands now combined into a joint fist and reeled backwards. With all his force, his fists plunged down upon the gash in the glass and shattered the shell.

Water came rushing forth from the hole and quenched the fire surrounding the massive ball. Soon, the entire glassy fabric was crumbling in on itself and Joshua found himself falling into the watery substance inside. He was now swimming inside the sun. Weird creatures that looked like hybrids between birds and fish swam past. A massive whale-like creature with the face of a goat went swimming past as well.

"Swim," he told himself. His body began picking up speed and the fish-birds became blurs as he sped past.

He had no idea where he was going, but he kept hearing the word "Anomie" in his head over and over again.

"Faster," he told his arms, and his arms obediently started pedaling in a swift windmill motion. He became a human jet engine flying towards the center of the massive sphere. He began to see a strange disturbance in the water getting closer and closer. It looked like a convergence of salt water and fresh water, or oil and water mixed together as one. Joshua realized the thing he was seeing was just a thin piece of fabric that was holding two separate worlds apart.

Within seconds of spotting this anomaly, his body began to slow down as it reached its destination.

"Anomie, Anomie, Anomie," his mind kept repeating this word, and it became like a massive resounding gong inside his head. His arms stopped paddling and clung to his sides. His body flipped backwards and his legs tightened up as they aimed towards the disturbance in the ocean of the sun.

Like a bullet merging with flesh, his legs penetrated the irregularity in the water, and he shot through it with intense speed ripping the delicate barrier between both worlds. He emerged into open sky, and fell through midair as the tear he had just made reformed itself behind him. He fell through the clear blue sky, heading like a freight train towards the surface. His body finally reached the grass covered ground and his feet dug into it cleaving out a crater ten feet deep into the earth. He crawled out completely unharmed, however, finding himself now in a beautiful garden.

Sitting next to a large patch of flowers was what looked like a little girl with a bright red bow in her hair. Joshua's body walked towards her, this time without his permission. It was strange that in dreams you are in complete control, without really having any control at all. The little girl shuffled a bit as Joshua neared her, and her head turned around to face him.

Looking at Joshua was not the face of a little girl, however, but of an old woman in a little girl's body.

"Welcome back," the little old-girl said with the voice of a seven-year old. "I thought we had almost lost you, my son."

She stood up and began walking towards Joshua who was now standing completely motionless before her.

"Hello, Anomie," Joshua's mouth said without his control, as if his mind was now just a spectator in his own body. He was watching a play that he had no say in, the words had already been written, and his body was merely one of the players.

"Where is your mother, Anomie?" he asked.

"Today, mother died, Joshua. Or maybe yesterday, I don't know. All I know is that you were almost lost to us. We don't care. It's good that you're back. You are free to go your own way. Follow what I say, as usual of course," the little old-girl replied.

"May I have one of these flowers, Anomie?" Joshua asked.

"All things are lawful here. You can do what you like," said Anomie.

Joshua watched as his body picked up a flower and crumbled it in his hand. His body then started stomping the flowers, and both he and Anomie laugh as he does so.

"Is it not wonderful Joshua? Is it not terrible, this place?" Anomie grabbed Joshua's hand, and began leading him through the flowerbed. Both stomping as they walked.

"Indeed, both, Anomie," Joshua agreed.

"What would you like to do next my little Joshua?" she asked.

"I am bored, I am tired of this dreaming within dreams," Joshua replied. "Why is all of this happening? What is my purpose in life?"

"There is no 'why' Joshua, there is only nothingness. Nothing is better than Heaven, and a cupcake is better than nothing. Therefore, a cupcake is better than Heaven. Trying to find meaning in a meaningless life will get you nowhere. You would be better off here picking flowers and eating cupcakes, then trying to find meaning."

Joshua sat in his seat of the mind and watched all of this happen. He kept screaming out what to say, what to do as he had done before; but it was no use, his body just kept on its predetermined path. He knew that what Anomie was saying was not right, it may have previously been what he thought on earth, but after everything that he had seen and heard, now he knew better. There was meaning; there was purpose and he sure as Lovelight knew that Heaven was way better than cupcakes! All of these thoughts he screamed forth until his brain was sore from screaming. His body was now like a stubborn child, going its own path with total disregard for authority. His mind was stronger now than it had been before, but his body was just as weak.

Joshua watched as Anomie's face started to change from that creepy, old smile into a slight frown. He did not know what was causing this change in emotion so quickly, but he soon caught on when he realized that his own face was changing shape as well. The muscles in his face began to show rage. Not that the rage of his mind was finally getting through, but as if his body was starting to reject this place as well.

This was not your ordinary sort of rage mind you. No, this was a "I want you dead and gone," sort of rage.

Anomie took a step back as Joshua's body took a step forward.

"Joshua, what is it my love?" Anomie asked, her old voice now quivering.

Joshua opened his mouth and spoke, quiet at first, but then it grew louder and louder until it took on a shape and form and was like an unstoppable force spearing into Anomie.

"No, no, no, NO, NO, NO!" Joshua's body screamed.

Anomie, now backpedaling her feet faster than a politician who had made a slip of the tongue– found Joshua's body creeping forward faster than before.

"NO, NOT ANYMORE, YOU ARE NOT MY LOVE!" Joshua barked these words straight into the little old-girl's face. Spit flying, and his face bright red with blood.

Joshua's body had gone off script, and Anomie, like any good director, wanted to yell "cut" and try it all over again, but it was too late. Joshua's body pounced onto the little girl's, and now had its hands wrapped tightly around her wrinkled old throat.

"Joshua ... not supposed to be like ... this ... he won't let you escape ... not for what you have done ... Lani ...," she struggled out.

The creature known as Anomie toppled to the ground, eyes rolling back in her skull, and then was no more. Joshua rolled off the body as it burst into flames, and with it, the garden as well. Joshua sat surrounded by the flaming garden. His body and mind now unified once more, he remembered everything in a flash. He remembered Apostolos, and Skinless, and of how he had fallen asleep under the Ghost Tree's branches. He had slept enough. It was time to stop dreaming.

8

THE DAY THE GHOST TREE FELL

JOSHUA AWOKE TO FIND himself back in the forest of Absalom. He rubbed the sleep out of his eyes, wondering how long he had been out. None of that mattered though. All that mattered now was escaping from this forest (as well as from the Ghost Tree's grasp).

Joshua turned and looked up at the giant tree, searching for any sign of movement. Any swaying limb or moving branch would have been enough to tell him to remain still, but there was nothing.

"Perhaps the tree sleeps," he wondered, "perhaps." Regardless of it really being asleep or not, he was gonna get out while the gettin' was good. Being surrounded by the Ghost Tree on all sides made him feel like a baby lamb in a lion's cage. And all he knew was that in the forest, the mighty forest, the lion was sleeping tonight. Joshua rose to his feet and kicked his legs into gear. Sprinting as fast as he could back to the straight path.

He was just a few yards away from the path and each step brought him closer to freedom. Joshua was just a hop, skip, and jump away now. But suddenly, that old familiar sound of branches crackling came to his ears, and he turned just in time to see a giant branch swooping in to take his head clean-off. Joshua ducked and dove, just narrowly avoiding the branch's grasp. He was grateful that he had decided to continue playing football into college, as his bobbing and weaving skills came rushing back to him.

"Where are you going Joshua!" the tree shouted. The sound of many voices boomed throughout the forest; the Ghost Tree had awakened. Another branch shot out from the ground and wrapped itself around Joshua's leg. He scrambled across the forest floor, grabbing at anything to keep him anchored, anything to prevent him from being lifted into the air by the Ghost Tree's branch. He reached for one of the many axe handles strewn about the landscape, realizing for the first time why there were so many there in the first place. Others had tried to kill this thing before. He was determined to not fail where others had though. He would topple the Ghost Tree.

Reaching out, he grabbed one of the handles. It immediately broke and crumbled in his hand. He flipped over and kicked at the branch, the chains around his arms and legs growing heavy and making his escape difficult. It was as if the chains were in cahoots with the Creature. The Tree yanked harder, and Joshua slipped off his shoe and wriggled his leg loose. Joshua barrel rolled around the forest floor, dodging every branch that would pound the ground around him, all the while grabbing at axe handles hoping for one intact. Every once in a while, the Ghost Tree would land a lucky hit, resulting in Joshua getting the wind knocked out of him, or, slicing through his skin.

Joshua, now frantically grabbing at handles had gone through six with no luck. Laughing, the Ghost Tree stretched forth his branches once more, this time grabbing both of Joshua's legs. He lunged forth for another axe handle, all the while his chains thudding against the forest floor. Knowing this was his last chance, he gripped the handle before him with all his might. This handle, however, was heavier than the others; this one had a head to match the handle. A smile came across Joshua's bloodied face as he grasped the handle tightly just as The Ghost Tree lifted him high into the air.

The Tree swung Joshua outwards, and the face in the Tree began to open its mouth wide. A giant hole appeared in the middle of the tree, and what was originally just a tree hollow, was now a gaping mouth. The bark curved in around it giving the hole the appearance of having teeth. The tree swung the branch inward and flung Joshua head first towards the void of the great tree's mouth.

Joshua reeled the axe back in midair and swung as hard as he could right before he reached the gaping mouth. The axe head buried itself deep into one of the Ghost Tree's eyes. Joshua's legs swung into the creature's mouth, and then came swinging back out just in the nick of time before the hollow closed in pain. Joshua heard a shriek come from every tree in the forest, and the trees trembled and moaned. A rainstorm of leaves came showering down upon the forest floor, and the Ghost Tree began spitting out red sap from its mouth. Joshua kicked his legs against the tree and wrenched the axe head out. He fell to the ground and began his assault on the tree's base.

The axe cut through the tree like a hot-knife through Styrofoam. Joshua could tell this axe was made specifically for this purpose; to fell the Ghost Tree. He had not noticed the axe at first, and wondered if it hadn't been placed there by someone while he was sleeping. The enormous tree with all of its thousands of voices cried in agony as Joshua sliced through the trunk. His mother's voice, emanating from the tree's mouth, echoed throughout the forest. His father was heard screaming in pain, begging Joshua to stop his onslaught, and for a brief second he actually considered the proposition; it was very brief. The Tree made the grave error of taking the voice of Joshua's brother next, however. For this voice; Joshua would only swing harder. Branch after branch came flailing towards Joshua, but each one was met with the head of the axe. Red sap gushed from the bark of the great Tree with each strike from the axe, and the mouth sputtered and gargled out each word, all the while coughing up red sap that went spilling out onto the forest floor.

Joshua had done a lot of damage to the trunk of the tree, but it was time to end this. He swung the axe with all his might and dug it in the forehead of the Beast. With one last scream, the Ghost Tree gave up the ghost. The tree once large and powerful, now drooped like a weeping willow, and eventually, snapped and toppled to one side. Joshua was covered in red sap and leaves, making him look like a distant cousin of Swamp Thing.

Joshua fell backwards, sweating, panting, and exhausted from his battle. He looked over at the axe handle grasped in his hands and noticed the word "VERITAS" inscribed on the side. The truth did indeed cut deep; the bloody stump sticking out of the earth was now proof of that fact.

Joshua struggled to his feet–leaving the axe behind just in case the Ghost Tree ever recovered. The roots of the wicked run deep and he doubted whether he had actually defeated the Beast permanently. A minor victory is all this was, he thought. He walked towards the narrow path, and before he knew it, he had arrived at the forest's edge.

Joshua stumbled out of the woods, covered in red tree sap, and his own red sap poured out of cuts and gashes all over his body. Leaves from the forest had hitched a ride via the sap, and Joshua struggled to keep his clothes from sticking to his body. The hair on his head now glued together in tiny clumps from dried sap, and dried blood. He looked down at his appearance, and for the first time in his life he did not care what he looked like. He was only happy to be alive.

"Am I alive?" he thought to himself with a small laugh. This question seemed to be a recurring one in this new-found world of his, and he began to understand that all would be answered when he reached the Master.

Now, out of the forest and standing at the border of a large field, Joshua noticed something approaching him from the other side. He gazed off into the distance and saw the figure of a man running towards him waving his arms; it was Apostolos. A welcome sight indeed.

PART THREE:

TRIUMPH

1

You Would Never Break the Chain

"Joshua! Oh my friend, my dear friend!" Apostolos cheered.

Within seconds, Apostolos was upon him and had grabbed Joshua in his arms–tossing him up in the air.

"It is a blessed day indeed to see you out of that forest!" Apostolos said. "Many I have led to the mouth of that wood, but few have I greeted on the other side. It is surely only because of the Master that you stand here before me; and thanks be for that! I am sorry that I have been so short with you up until this point, but you see, I could only show you the path, my Master however, must take whom He chooses *along* that path," He continued.

"Please sit down Joshua, for I have much to say, and very little time to say it. Lanirche is very unhappy with us as I am sure you can imagine. My Master dealt a decisive blow against him, and with you and many others now taken from his grasp, he will be after you with his entire force. You must prepare for the coming trials, Joshua. You must be rid of those chains, so that you may be able to walk the narrow path with a guide. I know this is a lot to take in, but you have been called for a purpose."

"The forest was treacherous, but what lies ahead will be even more so. Look around the outside of this path, Joshua, what is it you see?"

Joshua turned where he was sitting and surveyed the surrounding field. Littered around the ground were arrows. Some were simply dug into the ground while others were embedded in human skeletons, long since decayed.

"What you see around you are the arrows of enmity," Apostolos explained. "Lanirche waits in his high tower for the ones who would venture out of these woods. Like a master archer he draws back his bow striking down those not strong enough to dodge his attacks. Let these remains be a reminder to you always of what can happen when you drop your guard against him. Now, as far as your chains. Do you see that large hill behind me?" Apostolos asked, scratching his beard.

Joshua tilted his head, scanning the distance for what Apostolos had mentioned. Piercing the horizon was an enormous hill at least 500-hundred feet tall and as steep as any hill he had ever seen.

"That is the Koimeterion," Apostolos explained. "It is where our Master did a powerful and wonderful thing; it is where death was murdered. You must climb that hill, for it is at the top that you will be freed from your chains. After you have done this, we will make camp and rest for a time."

Joshua sat for a while and absorbed everything his friend had said. After defeating the Ghost Tree, he was ready for anything. He was tired of the burden of these chains, tired of the life he used to live, and most of all, tired of running from his problems. It was time to kick the devil in the teeth.

As if responding to his thoughts of demonic dentistry, a whistling noise came swishing past his ears. Quicker than a flash of light, Apostolos' hand shot out and grabbed an arrow in mid-flight, just inches from Joshua's head.

"Go quickly, Joshua! The Ghost Tree has told Lanirche of your triumph! Quickly to the hill!" Apostolos shouted.

Joshua sprung to his feet, just as a volley of arrows whizzed past and dug themselves in the ground where he had just been sitting. Running as fast as his injured body would carry him; he evaded the arrows with that same football-like juking that he had used back in the forest. One came whizzing in and grazed the side of his leg cutting a small gash that brought him stumbling to the ground.

"Get up, Joshua. Get up," he said to himself. Joshua returned to his feet. An arrow buzzed past his left ear, and he caught himself wanting to swat it away as if it were an angry bee.

He continued running, getting farther and farther out of range with each step towards the massive hill in front of him. Soon, the arrows began to fall just short of him and he realized he was finally in the clear. He stopped to catch his breath, and noticed that he was at the base of the hill called Koimeterion. He took one last look up at the tower of "Lanirche, Inc.", far off in the distance, imagining Lanirche beating his minions high atop the tower. He pictured Skinless' face scowling as he watched Joshua stride away virtually unscathed.

Slowing his stride, he approached the massive hill before him. He was humbled by the Koimeterion, overwhelmed by the sheer size of the hill he must now climb. Joshua moved his right foot forward, immediately noticing the chains around that ankle grow weighty. He took another step, this time with his left foot. Again, the weight of the chains grew more prominent.

With each continuing step the weight of the chains increased and the shackles dug deeper into the skin around Joshua's ankles and wrists. The hill began to grow steeper as he clambered up the side, and he now had to resort to climbing on all fours like a child. He eventually reached a point where the ground began to level out, and found that at this new incline he could actually jog with little effort. A wooden cross came into view at the top of the hill, and he reckoned that this must be the destination that Apostolos had intended. At the sight of the cross, however, the chains now began to rattle uncontrollably.

Joshua worked to steady his arms and legs which were now vibrating violently. He continued up the hill, feeling the resonating chains pulsing through his body. It was difficult yes, but he had survived many an earthquake in his day, and this was a cake walk compared to those. The chains themselves now chose a different tactic, since the uncontrollable shaking wasn't working. They began to dig themselves into the ground. With each stride, he found himself yanking the chains from the dirt.

Each time the chains would hit soil, they would take root in hopes of anchoring him down. Joshua knew that if the chains were fighting even harder now, his freedom must rest at the top of the hill, somewhere near that cross. The chains started burying themselves even deeper. With each step, he now found himself having to throw his entire body weight to release the chains from the earth. The chains were vibrating so intensely that they started to give off a loud high-pitched noise. The sound made it seem as if the chains themselves were screaming in terror. It was as if they knew they were on death row, and that the cross was their lethal injection.

Within less than a hundred feet away from the cross now, Joshua's ascent suddenly came to an abrupt halt. The chains were now heavier than he was, and so rooted in the ground that any further progress was like trying to swim upstream with blocks of cement tied to your legs. He fell to his knees and began to cry. Sweat, mixed with blood from his wounds, dripped into his mouth and the taste of tinfoil intermingled with salt came to him as he spat into the dirt.

"What now?" he asked himself. He would never turn back and go down the hill, never after what he now knew. He would just have to sit here until someone came and helped him, or until he rotted away. He turned over and lay on his back. Looking up, he saw that there was an actual sun now (not just that strange light as before outside his cell) and its intense heat beat down upon his face.

He laid there for a while, maybe hours. He watched the sun move slowly across the sky, and slowly with it went his hopes of ever being rid of his chains. He noticed, however, that as the sun crept through the sky, something else was creeping towards him. The shadow of the cross was gradually moving closer-and-closer to him along the grass.

"Are you kidding me!" he cried aloud. "I came this far only to be teased with my redemption! Only to glimpse a shadow of what I could have had!" Joshua threw his head backwards against the grass as tears came flowing down his cheeks.

As the sun moved in the heavens, Joshua could feel the heat begin to subside. Soon the light would be gone, and he would be left only with darkness, his old friend. He closed his eyes as the blinding light of the sun faded away and the coolness of the shadow began to pass over him. The very second the shadow had touched his left arm, the chains began to shake so violently that anyone looking on would have thought Joshua was seizing. He felt a lightness come over him as he lay convulsing, and he understood all at once that the shackles around his wrists and ankles had weakened.

Taking the opportunity given to him, he rose to his feet and dashed upward. Sprinting now in the path of the shadow as it moved slowly across the ground. The chains were helpless, they had lost all their power in the shade of this weapon. He was just a few feet away now from the foot of the cross. Joshua dove for it with all his might and threw his arms around the wooden base. No sooner had he done so, than he heard a clicking noise and the shackles fell from his body and burst into dust.

He held onto the base of the cross like he was holding onto a loved one, and the words of Martin Luther King Jr. came to his head ...

"Free at last! Free at last! Thank God Almighty, we are free at last!"

2

I WILL NOT DIE BUT LIVE

"WELCOME TO THE KOIMETERION." Joshua released the wooden trunk, and flung himself backwards as he searched for the source of this new voice.

"Up here you idiot!"

Joshua leaned back on the palms of his hands and looked up, noticing only a large black cloak that had been nailed to the wooden cross on the opposite side of where he had grabbed. The structure of a body was inside the cloth, but sticking out of the arm slots were not hands, but that of a human skeleton covered in what looked like a type of fungus. He gathered himself, and hopped to the other side of the cross. Not meaning to hop, but unable to help himself. He had never felt so free and light before, and he wondered if he might not float away if he weren't careful.

"I apologize for all of this rudeness. You know, not being there to escort you in person and all. As you can see, I have been a bit tied up," A wheezing laugh emanated from inside the cloak, and Joshua was quickly reminded of Skinless.

"It was so nice of you to come to *me* though! I must admit, I am a bit embarrassed to be seen like this. I have been like this for the good part of three days now, and my master Lanirche must be worried sick about me!" That same coughing sarcastic voice emerged from deep inside the cloak's hood, and the creature's arms and legs flailed and rattled from the laughter.

"Who are you? Better yet, what are you?" Joshua asked. "Is that you, Skinless? If it is you, then you know that my chains are now gone and you couldn't catch me even if you tried."

"Oh poor child, poor, poor child," the voice said, "you must be so frightened! All alone in this big ole' scawy wowld. And with nasty men trying to capture you. What's a poor little twenty-five year old like yourself to do!"

The creature, now clearly mocking Joshua, laughed once more, this time though it was not jovial; it was sinister. The laugh sent chills down Joshua's spine, and his flesh burst out into goose pimples.

"My name is Death, but you may call me Mors," the voice said. "It appears to me by your appearance, and by your question, that Skinless has been neglecting his duties. Never send a boy to do a man's job, am I right? Now, if you would be so kind as to let me down from here, I can be on my way and I can forget the whole telling Lanirche that I saw you thing. Sound like a deal?" Mors asked.

"I am not into making deals with the devil, Mors. Surely, if you are the all-powerful 'Death' you can let yourself down, yes?" Joshua, now clearly enjoying being the one in charge, openly mocked Mors.

Mors hung still for a few seconds as the wind began to pick up. The cloak started to swish back and forth in the breeze. A large gust came down over the top of the hill, and then blew upwards revealing the face of Mors; the face of Death. This was nothing like Joshua had ever imagined, or even seen in artist's depictions of the "Grim Reaper". Mors' flesh had long since decayed, and now where flesh should be was just rot.

In the eye sockets were two human's eyes, one red and one blue. The skull was like a human's as well, but badly cracked and misshapen. Bugs poured forth in a stream of blood and mucus that gushed from what was left of the creature's nasal cavity. Mors stared straight at Joshua and grinned. Some of his teeth were missing, but the ones that were not were blackened and yellow. This was death incarnate, the most foul, hideous thing that anyone could ever see or imagine.

"You would mock the Mors?" Death asked. "No man can escape me, Joshua; I have reigned ever since Adam, the first man, and will rule until the last man on earth departs. It is true that I have been bruised by the Prophet, but I will heal. I endure, Joshua; I will be the Prophet's last enemy. So yes, I may not be able to let myself down, but I am still indeed powerful. SO WATCH YOUR MOUTH!"

All manner of fluid and night crawlers came spitting out of Mors mouth, as his grin turned into a scowl, screaming these last words. Joshua fell to the ground at the sudden jolt of Mors' body.

"That's quite enough out of you Mors," spoke a familiar voice.

Joshua turned his head, startled at first, and then overjoyed to see his brother and friend Apostolos. Apostolos walked over to Joshua and reached out his right hand to help him to his feet.

"Ah, Apostolos, my old friend!" said Mors jovially. "It has been a long time since I have seen the man whose looks rival even my own!"

Apostolos just smiled his usual friendly smile, and carefully walked around the backside of the cross.

"The Prophet sits in His Father's house Mors," Apostolos said. "You have lost, and Lanirche has been fatally wounded through your defeat. He will not be happy to see you I am afraid. I only free you now, because your end is now certain. My Master will swallow you up entirely in His final victory which is soon to come. Now go and run back to your master. Tell him Apostolos says hello."

Apostolos reached up and touched the back of the tree. The nails chaining the creature to the cross shot out like bullets, and Mors fell to the ground, as more fluid came pouring forth from every orifice on his body. Cockroaches poured from his sleeves and covered the ground, scattering in search of darkness. Mors recovered, and got to his feet. No sooner had he balanced himself than he was lunging straight for Joshua. Joshua reared back ready to defend himself. He had faced Death so many times already that this was becoming almost a sort of tradition for him in this world.

Death was almost upon him, but just as Mors was about to strike, the creature's body was propelled backwards by an unseen force. The back of Mors spine hit the wooden cross and wrapped itself around the wooden pole like an old snap bracelet. Mors' bones sounded like a small tree being bent in half as they hit the solid wood.

"You will find that you have some restrictions, old boy," Apostolos said. "Joshua is one of the Master's chosen, and you have no hold over him. Now do as I said before and leave this place."

Mors needed no second telling this time. He stretched himself out, popped his back and neck, and within seconds was back on his feet bolting off in the direction of Lovelight. Joshua looked off in the direction to which Mors was running and noticed the giant skyscraper that was "Lanirche, Inc." so lit up that it looked as if it were on fire.

"How are you feeling, brother? It is good to be free of those chains, yes?" Apostolos asked.

"Apostolos, thank you," Joshua replied. "I had never felt the weight of these chains until you showed me, and I never knew how free I could feel until the Master released me! This is all very new and frightening. I have so many questions!"

"There will be time for questions later when you reach the Master's house, brother," Apostolos answered. "For now, we must make camp and get some rest. You have quite a journey ahead of you tomorrow."

"Please, just one question before we go. Is my body dead; am I really dead back on Earth?" Joshua asked.

"We were all once dead Joshua, but the Spirit has made us alive. But to answer your question; I am afraid the Master alone holds that knowledge. But I do know this, you are exactly where the Master wants you to be and that is all that matters." Joshua lowered his head. He had hoped for a clear cut answer; he had hoped for a simple yes or no. Apostolos put his arm on Joshua's shoulder, seeing that he was saddened by this answer.

"I wish I could tell you more Joshua, but I can only guide you on the path the Master has set before you. Everything else is in His hands. Here, let me show you something that will hopefully make things clearer."

Apostolos walked to the wooden cross and motioned for Joshua to come closer.

"Look at the cross that stands before you Joshua," Apostolos said pointing to the wooden beams.

Joshua walked over to the cross sticking out high atop the Koimeterion. As he drew closer, he noticed something which he had mistaken beforehand as a design or pattern, realizing now that is was no pattern but instead words carved into the timber. He reached out his hands and followed the etchings with his fingertips. He saw millions of names carved into the wooden beam. Not carved by any tool made by human hands. These were words carved by sacrifice. He read some of the names not recognizing any, and then he saw it. His heart pounded hard in his chest as his fingers moved slowly over the words: Joshua Hawkins.

"Your debt has been paid my friend," Apostolos said smiling. "If you look long enough you will find my name written upon that tree as well. Those are the names of the Master's children, Joshua. Lanirche would love nothing more than to scratch your name off that post. Not just your name, but every name. This is why Mors could not harm you. This doesn't mean that Lanirche will stop trying to capture you though. That is why you must now rest and prepare for what lies ahead."

Joshua removed his hands from the cross and turned around with tears in his eyes and a smile upon his face.

"Let us rest then, my friend," Joshua said. "I will continue on the narrow path, and seek the Master's house. Nothing will stop me. Not Lanirche, Mors, or even the gates of Lovelight can stand against me now, for I am lighter and surer than I have ever been. I will not die but live!"

3

SILENCE IN THE WAITING

NAIL SALON BACK IN CHICAGO ...

"What do you mean my boy is hurt?" Ms. Hawkins was having her nails done when a call came in from the police station. "Is he going to be okay? What happened?" She frantically screams into the phone as the poor little Asian woman doing her nails gets kicked in the face and starts yelling in her own language. "Have you called Joshua's father yet? Where did you take him? Okay, I am on my way." Elizabeth Hawkins (Joshua's real mother) runs out the salon door still donning curlers and with only one hand of fingernails painted. She whistles and waves as a small yellow cab pulls up. Elizabeth hurriedly jumps in and barks out an address.

"Step on it! My little boy is hurt!" Elizabeth yells.

"Lady, if I had a dollar for every time somebody said 'step on it,' I would be rich," the cabby remarked. "I'll go as fast as I can though, so cool those jets."

The cabby weaves in and out of traffic, running red lights where possible, and after the longest nine minutes of Elizabeth's life, they arrive safely at the hospital.

"Thank you, and keep the change!" Elizabeth says, throwing money through the window.

The cabby counts out over a hundred bucks worth of fare, and decides that from now on he is only going to stop for crazed frantic mothers.

Elizabeth runs for the sliding glass doors of the ER. Her heel catches the curb, and she is sent sprawling forth onto the sidewalk. The entire contents of her purse come stumbling out, and she scrambles to gather them back quickly into their three-hundred-dollar-designer-home. Elizabeth pushes past a nurse, nearly knocking her on the floor, and rushes for the reception desk.

"My son! Where is he?" Elizabeth demanded.

"Ma'am, I am afraid I am not a clairvoyant," said the nurse very snarkily. "What is your son's name?"

"His name is Joshua," Elizabeth answered, "Joshua Hawkins. I received a call from the police saying he had been shot. Please tell me where I can find my little boy!"

"He is currently in ICU. Head down this hall and take a left. Follow the signs. You can't miss it," the nurse replied, feeling somewhat ashamed at her initial tone towards the woman.

Elizabeth booked it down the hall, removing her heels this time in order to avoid another spill. She slid around the corner in a very Risky Business-esque manner, and arrived at the ICU desk.

"Yes, hello. I am Joshua Hawkins' mother. Can you tell me if he is alright?" she asked the woman behind the counter.

"He is stable at the moment," the nurse replied, "but he is in critical condition. Doctor Gonzalez has been waiting for you. Let me send for him."

The nurse picks up the phone, dials an extension, and within seconds a man in a white doctor's robe comes rushing down the hallway.

"Hello Mrs. Hawkins," the doctor said, offering his hand to the frantic mother.

Elizabeth was surprised to find that doctor's hands not only heal, but comfort.

"I am going to get straight to the point. Your son is in critical condition. He has suffered two bullet wounds. Both went straight through without hitting any major organs—which was lucky—but upon hitting the pavement, he fractured his skull. There is a lot of swelling and a lot of blood loss. We are doing our best, but its touch and go at the moment. Your son is in a medically induced coma. We are waiting for the swelling to subside, but it is pressing down hard on his brain." Doctor Gonzalez stopped briefly, realizing he was still shaking the woman's hand which had now turned into a vice-grip.

"Things don't look good I am afraid. Do you understand what I am saying, Mrs. Hawkins?" the Doctor asked.

"That's miss Hawkins, and yes. Yes I think I do," she said with tears in her eyes. "You are telling me to say goodbye to the only son I have left. I understand very well."

4
AKELDAMA

"HERE WE ARE, JOSHUA. This is where we will make camp." Apostolos said, as the two men arrived at a bluff overlooking a deep valley. The walk from the koimeterion to here had only taken about thirty minutes, but after all the events of that day, Joshua was very tired and ready for sleep. The bluff at which the two men had now arrived had a large rock that shot out over the great canyon. The large expanse and sheer size of the valley reminded Joshua of the Grand Canyon. He had only been once in his life and was very young at the time, but he still remembered it like it was yesterday. This was one of the few family trips that he could remember as being fairly argument-free.

He recalled how his father had walked straight up to the ledge and stared fearlessly into the grand expanse. At the time, he saw his father as this herculean figure. A man who had looked fear in the eye, and overcome it. As he got older, however, he understood that his father was not courageous, but foolish to get so close to the edge. It was pompous, arrogant, and showed a complete disregard for his family. "What if something had happened to him?" he thought. "What if he had fallen over? I would have grown up without a father." But wasn't that the case anyways? Would things really have changed? Don't get me wrong, he wasn't a bad dad or anything. He never beat us or yelled or anything of that sort. He just was never there.

Joshua remembered seeing his father's face as he had turned around. As a child, Joshua mistook his father's face for confidence.

The image of his father's smug grin as he turned around burned in his mind. After everything he had experienced in this world, however, maybe he had been wrong all those years. Looking back, maybe his face wasn't smug or confident at all, maybe his face was terrified. His father wasn't staring into the great unknown out of arrogance, but out of fear.

Perhaps he was looking for an answer in that canyon. Maybe he was looking for his *own* way to get rid of his *own* chains. A way to conquer that which scared him most: The idea that somewhere out there in space or wherever, someone, or something, had carved that canyon. And knowing that no matter how successful he was in life, no matter how many deals he closed, or cars he bought, he would ever be able to escape whatever had imagined and created such a vast expanse.

Now, Joshua stared into the giant mouth of the canyon just as his father once had. He did not stare in fear or in arrogance though. Joshua stood in awe. Feeling very small, and very humbled at the immensity of the thing before him, and at the One who had dug it out with a mere thought.

"Beautiful, and yet terrible isn't it, Joshua?" Apostolos asked. "It is a paradox of nature that something like this can evoke two separate emotions at the same time. Our Master delights in paradoxes though. To Him, they are nothing more than basic math." Apostolos smiled as the sun sunk low over the horizon. "I have brought you here for a reason, Joshua. This valley is special. It has always known battle, and will continue to know battle until the Prophet returns to take up His rule. It is known as Akeldama, and its floors are stained red with blood," he continued.

"One day, the final battle will commence, and the red soil will be no more. It's name will no longer be Akeldama, but Padah. I only take you here so that you may understand the vastness of your journey. That what you do, and how you live, have massive ramifications. There was a battle in this very canyon for you, Joshua. Whether that makes sense to you now doesn't matter. What matters now is rest, for you will have your own battles in the coming day."

Apostolos finished, motioning for Joshua to sit. A campsite had already been prepared on the rock that jutted out over the canyon, and Joshua sat down on a log that had been placed on its side.

Apostolos leaned in to start a fire, and Joshua was surprised to see a shiny zippo lighter come out from underneath the man's robes. Night was now fully upon them, and the air had grown cold and damp. Joshua laid down next to the fire and gazed up into the night sky. The stars were shining bright, and they twinkled reminding Joshua of Christmas lights.

"How can I sleep on such a night as this, Apostolos," Joshua asked. "My heart is light, but also very anxious. Despite my exhaustion, I fear I will have difficulty sleeping."

"I understand completely," Apostolos said. "I once laid in the same spot that you now lay. But alas, you must sleep, my friend. Would it help if I sang? I don't sing very well, but I do sing often." Apostolos said laughing. "Wait, don't answer that. Once the idea comes to my mind, I can't be stopped. I apologize in advance for any wayward notes. They hopefully will return. That is of course if I don't venture too far from the melody."

The two men laughed together like old friends. Apostolos cleared his throat and Joshua closed his eyes leaning back using the log as a pillow. Apostolos began to sing. The voice that had previously scared Joshua when he was imprisoned by Skinless, now soothed him. It was a song of woe, a song of future things, and a song of victory.

The multitude stood strong and fast,
Their armor a mirror for the sun.
Michael leads the charge with a blast,
His courage equaled by none.

The flaming swords are drawn,
The enemies they jeer;
Their gnashing teeth are no match,
For the weapons here.

Lanirche rides in on dragon back,
The creature black as soot.
Michael meets this devils path,
And leaves ground underfoot.

The armies clash and bodies fall,
The blessed swing and hack.
The damned meet the blessed attack,
And push and shove right back.

Mors soon joins the army damned,
Mount on skeletal steed.
He opens up his cursed mouth,
In hopes to devour the freed.

Michael lets out a cry of praise,
The nightmare army quakes.
The winged men swooping down,
Leave nothing in their wake.

Lanirche enraged at the praise,
Kicks his dragon's sides;
Intent to kill the one who fights
For the Master's bride.

Michael brave and striking fast,
Meets dragon in the air.
Lanirche swings strong but cannot best,
The swordsman's mighty flair.

The dragons heart bonds with blade,
Its rider is now thrown;
As through Lanirche's fingers slip,
His dream of seizing the throne.

Mors comes riding to his aid,
Stilling his master's fall;
They both ride off in fevered haste,
Fleeing the bloody brawl.

Michael sounds the victory trump,
The cursed cower in fear;
Watching as their leaders run,
The blessed army cheers.

The skirmish has been won this day,
The final battle nears;
When Lanirche will rear his head once more,
And Mors will too appear.

On that day the Prophet shall ride,
On a horse white as snow.
A sword shall spring from his lips,
And cut His enemies low.

All will bow before the King,
In Heaven and on Earth.
Lifting high the One who gives,
All His children new birth.

Apostolos finished his song, and looked on at a now snoring Joshua. He stoked the fire, adding a few more logs before he too laid down and closed his eyes. Somewhere deep in the bowels of Lovelight, however, Lanirche wasn't sleeping. He was wide awake and planning his next move, and oh what a move it was.

5
SIGHTS AND SOUNDS

THE NEXT DAY, JOSHUA AWOKE to the sound of battle. Swords clashing, arrows swishing, and bodies thudding. The sound was coming from deep within the canyon. He gathered himself, rubbed the matter out of his eyes, and crawled to the edge of the bluff in hopes to spy the source of all this racket. Apostolos was still fast asleep, and as Joshua crawled passed his body, he decided that it would be better not to wake him up if there was no cause for alarm.

Joshua peaked out over the ledge. His eyes and nose the only thing visible over the ledge, making him look like Kilroy. Looking down into the valley, he expected to see two large armies going at it in full force, but instead, saw nothing. He noticed that the dark red ground of the valley below seemed to be growing darker by the second. He pulled back from the edge of the cliff, and walked back to his rock-bed deciding it would be best to just wait until Apostolos woke up to ask him about the invisible battle.

Joshua soon began to doze off, and just as he was about to fall back to sleep, he jerked to life at the sound of Apostolos' booming voice. The man had one volume: hurricane force winds.

"Good morning!" Apostolos shouted. He was obviously a morning person, the type of person that Joshua usually didn't get along with.

"I hope you slept well. I know this rock is no spring mattress, but I have always found it to be more than suitable for a night's rest."

"It was fine. Thank you." Joshua replied absent-mindedly. "Apostolos, do you hear that noise? Please tell me it's not just me.

I am just starting to feel semi-sane again." Apostolos laughed at Joshua's question and then answered.

"No my friend, it is not just you. I too hear it. That sound is the sound of battle. Did you not listen to my song last night? Was I that terrible?" Joshua had heard a few verses, but had soon thereafter dozed off. He was too embarrassed to admit it with words, but his facial expression gave it away.

"No worries," Apostolos said. "I am just surprised that you could actually sleep while I warbled on!" He said laughing as Joshua waited impatiently for his answer.

"Oh yes, the noise, sorry," Apostolos said composing himself. "There is a battle raging right now that we can't see, Joshua. Down in that valley they are fighting for someone. Someone who was just like you. When that battle ends, I must leave you and attend to whomever it is that they are fighting for."

"You can't come with me? But what if I need your help?" Joshua asked.

"You will be fine, Joshua," Apostolos answered. "The Master has provided you with a guide already who is far superior than I could ever be. Follow the narrow path. Resist Lanirche and he will flee from you. We will meet again, do not fear." Apostolos finished speaking just as the sound of battle ended and the sound of singing came rising from the valley below.

"That's my cue," said Apostolos.

"Thank you for all you have done for me, friend," Joshua said, lifting his arm out to shake Apostolos' hand. Apostolos looked at the young man's hand and smiled as he opened his arms and pulled Joshua close. The two men hugged and said their goodbyes. Apostolos headed off back in the direction of the Forest of Absalom, and waved one last time before completely fading off into the horizon.

Joshua took a few minutes to tend to his wounds which were all scabbing up rather nicely, and the ones that weren't scabbed at least had the blood coagulated. He brushed the dust off his clothes and took one last look off into the canyon before he headed back for the narrow path. The place in which the two men had slept was only a few feet from the road, so there was little difficulty finding his way back.

The walk was much easier now that he no longer bore the marks of a slave, and as he walked, he examined his wrists where the chains had once been. His wrists were bruised and badly scarred from where the chains had dug in over the years. He knew that even though the chains were gone, he would still bear the scars forever. They were gone, but not forgotten.

A tiny pain shot through the back of his head, and a quick rub took it away as it had done in the past.

"Must be from the rock-bed," he thought.

He continued walking down the path for what seemed like miles. The heat of the sun at its pinnacle, pelting down upon him. He passed a river and noticed that he was no longer hungry or thirsty as he had been before in the Forest of Absalom. The narrow path cut right through the river, and there was a tiny little wooden bridge that passed over it. The bridge was antiquated and decrepit, and it looked as if it was held together only by prayer. Joshua ran as fast as he could over the bridge and jumped for the other side. To his astonishment, the bridge stood firm and didn't even seem to notice that someone had just ran over it.

Hours passed as Joshua continued down the path. He walked by many strange sights and sounds along his way. There was a side path that appeared to have been man-made. This path had a sign that Joshua read as he passed:

City of Vanity Fair This Way

This may have been a shortcut, but Joshua had learned his lesson twice already when it came to straying from the path. He walked by without a second glance.

Along the way, he also passed by a large mine. Outside of the mine was a man who called out to him.

"Come traveler! There is wealth to be had here! You could be richer than your wildest dreams!"

"No thank you, friend!" Joshua yelled back. "I must stay on this path, for my reward is far greater than wealth! Why don't you come join me instead?" Joshua asked.

"I have already been on that path!" the man shouted. "I am tired of walking it though! I will take my fortune now! And you should as well!" Joshua looked off at the man in sadness. Wishing he could convince him to retake the path once more.

"Is there nothing I can say that will persuade you otherwise?!" Joshua pleaded.

"I am afraid not! I am rich beyond my wildest dreams! Come join me!" the man once again insisted. Joshua, knowing that this would just be a circular argument, continued walking as the man continued shouting after him.

Joshua pressed on, passing various monuments along his way. There was a white statue of a woman that he saw in the middle of a field. He passed by another statue, this one of a man, however. On its base were the words, "Agnostos Theos." As he walked on, he wondered who had erected such odd vestiges. Perhaps other travelers before him. Men and women not unlike himself perhaps. He also wondered how many of them had gone astray. How many had chosen other paths that they thought would take them to the Master's kingdom. Joshua knew better now though, he knew that there was only *one* true path; only one way to the King.

The path ahead of him steadily grew narrower (which was quite a task for a road already titled, "the narrow path"). There was a decently large mountain that he had noticed off in the distance for some time, but he realized now that the path was curving towards it. Coming to the foot of the mountain, he saw that the narrow path led to the mouth of a cave. The cave was pitch black, except for two large torches on either side of its entrance that vaguely revealed the path inside. Sitting on a rock outside the cave was an old man.

Joshua approached the mouth of the cave where the old timer sat.

"Who is there? What is your business here?" asked the old man.

"My name is Joshua, and I am following the narrow path. What is your name?" Joshua asked.

"My name is Tiriel," the man replied. "But you mustn't continue on that path. That road leads to the castle Carcosa, the home of the Yellow King. I doubt you will find him and his followers very accommodating." The man's voice was raspy and tired. His eyes were milky white, and Joshua recognized it as a seriously bad case of cataracts.

"I am afraid I must go through that cave. I must continue on the path," Joshua explained.

"So be it," the old man said. "But don't say I didn't warn you. You are just as foolish as my children! Disobeying the wisdom and advice of their elders. Well, be off with you then!"

Joshua watched as the old man lowered his head and started to snore heavily. He grabbed one of the torches that lined the sides of the cave and ventured in, unaware that Lanirche was waiting inside.

6
FAMILY REUNION

THE PASSAGE THROUGH THE TUNNEL was eldritch and dank. The torch flickered as the air grew thin. Joshua had done some bouldering in college, but he would have never referred to himself as a spelunker. Now, however, he found himself wishing he had taken it up as a hobby. He was shoving his body through nooks and cranny's that some children would have found difficult squeezes. This of course was not the worst part of the experience; the insects were.

The walls seemed alive as the creatures squirmed and wriggled across its surface. He was surrounded on all sides by creepy crawlers. Every once in a while, a few would drop, jump, bite, and slime onto Joshua's body. He was an intruder in their home, and they wanted him out almost as much as he wanted out.

The narrow passage opened up into an antechamber, but along the ground that same clear cut path was still visible. The kind of trail that is only made after years and years of travel. The torch was but a tiny light in this massive cathedral of stone, and it was the minority in this present darkness. Joshua treaded carefully, making sure at all times not to stray from the path. The rock underfoot began to close in on the path forming a rock bridge. It reminded Joshua of the invisible bridge from *Indiana Jones and the Last Crusade*, and right now, he knew that only the penitent man could pass.

He stepped gently onto the rocky structure, small pebbles cascading over the edge as he walked. He was tip-toeing now, thinking somehow that would help. He was like a tight rope walker–swaying left and right–and using his torch for balance. The end of the bridge was in sight, and he employed his classic "jump at the end of the bridge technique" in order to get across safely. In the same fashion as the bridge across the river though, jumping made no difference. The rock bridge stood firm with little regard for its traveler. The narrow path may have been difficult, but it would always be there for those who would choose to attempt it.

Joshua made it safely to the other side, feeling very proud of himself. The only thing missing from this picture, he thought, was a whip and a fedora. He continued on the path which now left the large antechamber, and made a sharp turn into a slender passage. Oh, how he had missed those crawling walls! Yeah … right.

The torch was starting to grow dim, and he knew it only had maybe an hour left of light in it before it died out. He would have to start moving faster and stop enjoying the "scenery". Joshua stopped caring about the bugs, and his body moved through the tiny passage like water. He was making up for lost time, and he wondered if he couldn't have already been out of the cave by now if he had just "manned up." The torch was fading faster than he had expected, and as it dimmed, so too did his courage.

Turning sharply and climbing over a large rock that had fallen in the path, Joshua saw before him a small amount of light emanating from the passage ahead.

"That has to be the exit," he thought. Adrenaline coursed through his veins at the idea of being bug free once again. Coming upon a passage heavily occupied by low-hanging stalactites, he found himself crawling towards the light. The stony spikes hung only inches from the floor, and Joshua had to resort to army crawling along the wet ground. He kicked hard along the floor, arm-over-arm, moving closer to the light. He accidentally slammed his leg against the side of the wall as a bug crawled up his thigh. He screamed in pain, his voice echoing up into the narrow corridor. The sound created a shock-wave effect, and stalactites began to rain down from the ceiling.

He pushed hard and fast against the cold ground, as a cave spike came crashing down in front of his face, missing his head only by centimeters. The stalactite burst into pieces, and the tiny calcified pebbles beat against his face. It was raining danger, and he felt as if he was being stoned for all of his sins as rock and spike shattered all around his prostrate body.

The stalactites subsided, but not before one last stony spike came crashing down slicing into his thigh. He rose to his feet, picked up the stalactite that had cut into his leg, and threw it down the long spiky-roofed passage with a barbarian yell. The stalactites shuttered as their fallen brother came hurdling back towards them in the darkness. They all evacuated their positions on the ceiling, and came shattering down upon the ground in a domino effect of noise and confusion.

Joshua had finally reached the turn that led to the light source. This part of the tunnel appeared to be man-made, and a ninety-degree angle pushed him left where the light was coming from. He turned, and much to his surprise, standing smack dab in the middle of the path was his "old pal" Lanirche.

"Out of the frying pan and into the fire," he thought.

"Joshua, my boy!" Lanirche said gleefully. "How happy I am to finally meet you in person!" The beautiful young Lanirche was upon Joshua before he even knew it and grabbed his hand firmly to shake.

"What a pleasant surprise this is! Meeting you in a place like this!" Lanirche said, giving a small laugh.

"I wish I could say the same," Joshua replied.

"Now, now. No need to be rude," said Lanirche. "I told you in my letter that we would be meeting soon. You should have been expecting me."

"I thought you said it was a surprise to meet me here? Because, right now, it feels very planned," Joshua said skeptically.

"I am afraid I have not been honest with you, Joshua. I did indeed plan this meeting. I was just so anxious to meet you and apologize for everything that Skinless put you through. I hope there are no hard feelings," Lanirche said with a car salesman's smile.

"You mean to tell me you came here to apologize? You aren't here to try and capture me?" asked Joshua.

"And why would I do a thing like that?" Lanirche replied. "It seems that you are very set on following this little 'quest' of yours. Soon, you will realize just how foolish this whole thing is, and when you do, I will still be here waiting with open arms. Plus, just to show you how sincere I am, I thought I would offer you a gift as a means to reconcile things between us. Sound good?"

But that was the problem, it all sounded WAY too good to be true. Lanirche was the bad guy, Apostolos said so. But what if he wasn't as bad as he made him sound. What if he was just misunderstood? If he truly was being honest and he didn't come to capture him but to apologize, then where was the harm in that? After all, if Lanirche was what we call Satan in our world, maybe he was a lot like how Milton portrayed him in *Paradise Lost*—just a guy who wanted more than what he was offered.

"Alright," Joshua said, "but after you give me this gift or whatever, you have to allow me to continue on the path. Deal?"

"Deal," Lanirche said, as he reached out his hand to shake. Joshua took the man's hand, as the hint of a smirk appeared on his face.

"So what is this gift then? Let's have it so I can be on my way," Joshua said.

"It's hard to explain what it is, better to just show you. I can guarantee you though; it's something you have always wanted. Just this way, and don't worry, you don't have to step off your cute little path."

Lanirche led Joshua further down the tunnel, handing him a new torch as the two set off. They came to another large chamber, but this one was much smaller than the one before.

"Here we are," said Lanirche, "let me retrieve it for you." Lanirche bent low to the ground and began making a symbol in the dirt. Joshua had seen this done once before in Lovelight when Skinless had summoned the hell-hound. Lanirche finished his drawing and stepped back. The ground began to shake, and the place at which he had drawn the symbol collapsed in upon itself. Red light came shooting forth from the hole in the ground, and a noisome smell arose from within and filled the chamber. Lanirche walked over to the edge and reached his hand out over the top of the hole.

"Rise!" Lanirche shouted. A metal chain shot out of the opening, and Lanirche clasped it tightly in his hands. He started pulling the chain with little effort, the end of which coiled itself neatly on the ground behind him. He was clearly pulling something out of the hole, and whatever it was, (assumedly) was his "present." Lanirche looked like an ice fisher standing over the hole as he reeled in a prized catch.

He didn't have to pull long, however, as his "gift" for Joshua came to the surface of the hole. Attached to the end of the chain, was a man. A man who was hogtied, nude, and had his lips sewed shut. The man's head was shaved, and his face and body badly scarred. Even with all of these changes though, Joshua could still recognize the man chained before him; it was his brother, Marcus.

"Do you love it, or do you *love* it?" asked Lanirche. "It's just what you always wanted isn't it?" Joshua stood speechless, not knowing what to say. For years, Joshua had longed to see his brother face-to-face. Not just see him mind you, but kill him. Kill him for what he had done to him and that girl all those years ago.

"I know your heart's desire, Joshua, that's why I have arranged this little family get together. Here, this should help make things more clear." Lanirche reached out the hand not holding the chain, and opened his fist. In his palm a dagger materialized.

"Understand now?" Lanirche asked. Joshua understood all to well. He walked forward, stepping off the path. He took the dagger from Lanirche's hands and stared into the face of his brother. His eyes were sadder than he had remembered. Still blue and beautiful, but so very sad. Despite the scars as well, Marcus was still handsome. Ruggedly handsome now, but still not hard to look at. Joshua grasped the dagger tightly in his hands, his palm sweaty with anticipation.

"This is what you have always wanted," he told himself. "Just do it! Stab that bastard for everything he has done!" But he couldn't do it. Instead of anger, he felt only pity for his brother. And besides, wasn't the Abyss punishment enough?

"I can't," said Joshua.

"What do you mean you can't?" asked Lanirche. "I know you better than you know yourself. This is what you have wanted for years! Perhaps you just need a little motivation." Lanirche flicked his free hand over Marcus' mouth, and upon doing so his lips opened and he began to cough. Lanirche flicked his fingers once more, and this time words came from Marcus' lips.

"Glam … or … us … aint … it," he said, struggling out the words. Joshua cringed at the phrase, as visions of that fateful night flashed through his head.

"Remember that?" asked Lanirche. "One of my all-time favorite lines. I must admit, I quote it often in conversation." He laughed loudly, and his voice echoed throughout the chamber of the cave. Joshua looked down at the knife in his hand, and then looked at his brother. The two made eye contact, and out of Marcus' right eye came a single tear as his lips began to move.

"For … give," his voice said softly, as Lanirche shot out his leg breaking one of Marcus' ribs.

"That's enough out of you!" Lanirche barked. And that was enough; that was all Joshua needed to hear. His gaze turned from his brother to Lanirche. His hand was swift, and it helped that Lanirche was no mind reader. He was a gambler that worked on predictions. He could never know if his bets would pay off, or if he would end up going bust. This time, Lanirche the tempter, had rolled snake-eyes.

Joshua dug the dagger into Lanirche's stomach causing him to fall to his knees. His hand released the chain sending Joshua's brother plummeting down into the pit.

"You think this is the first time I have been stabbed?" Lanirche asked throwing his head back mockingly. "You can't kill me, you idiot."

"I don't need to kill you Lanirche," Joshua said. "Your fate has long been decided. I just need you out of my way."

Joshua dove for the coiled chain at Lanirche's feet, and quickly wrapped it around Lanirche's neck. Lanirche struggled to release himself, as the chain pulled tight, strangling him. The slack of the rope ended, and the weight of Marcus' body pulled Lanirche into the pit after him. Joshua walked to the edge of the gaping hole and watched Lanirche fall until he was no more than a black spot in a sea of red.

"I forgive you, Marcus," Joshua whispered. "I just hope you can forgive me."

7
THE CALL

A N OFFICE BUILDING IN DOWNTOWN CHICAGO ...

"Mr. Hawkins, your ex-wife is on the line." Jeremiah Hawkins was right in the middle of an important business meeting when his secretary ran in with the news. "She says it's an emergency."

"Alright," Jeremiah said, "I'll take the call in here. I apologize for the interruption, gentlemen. Should only be a second." Jeremiah walked embarrassed over to the phone sitting on his desk. "What could it be this time?" he thought. "The woman is already squeezing me for every penny I have, now what could she want?" Of course, she would call during the most important meeting of the year. A meeting that held the potential of making Mr. Hawkins an even richer man than he already was.

Three men sat around his conference table. They were from a company called *Mendacium,* and were interested in buying his company. They did this often, buying up all sorts of companies that sold various products. *Mendacium* had their hands in every honey pot in the world, and it was an honor if they sought out your business. Whatever they touched seemed to turn to gold. The best part of the whole thing was, they always allowed the owner to stay on as CEO of the company. They just sat back and ran it from the shadows with an invisible hand.

The men watched, annoyed that their precious time was being wasted by a call from this man's ex-wife. Jeremiah picked up the receiver and was met by the voice of his ex-wife sobbing.

"Jeremiah, it's Joshua!" The woman said, almost unintelligibly through snot and tears.

"He's hurt!"

"Calm down, Elizabeth. What's happened?" Jeremiah asked, attempting to stay cool and relaxed, not wanting to show any sign of weakness in front of his … guests.

"Joshua has been shot! Our little boy has been shot! Please hurry Jeremiah … he doesn't …'" The hysterical woman on the other line faded out as the sound of a loud thud came from her end. Many frantic voices poured from the receiver as Jeremiah tried his best to keep cool, faking a smile as he gazed at the three men. He mouthed a, "sorry about this" to the gentlemen, and returned to the phone.

"Hello, did I lose you? I couldn't quite make out what you said Elizabeth," Jeremiah replied.

"This is Doctor Gonzalez. Your wife has fainted, Mr. Hawkins."

"She's my ex-wife, and what exactly is going on?" Jeremiah whispered into the phone.

"Your son Joshua has been shot Mr. Hawkins. He suffered a severe skull fracture, and we are doing everything in our power to relieve the swelling and blood loss. I would advise you getting here immediately. He is currently in a medically induced coma, shutting down brain function in order to promote healing." Jeremiah received the news, as his Fonzie-like appearance quickly turned into a more Richie Cunningham-esque one.

"I'm on my way," Jeremiah said, with tears welling up in his eyes. He hung up the phone and turned to his three guests who all looked very surprised at what they just heard him say.

"You are not leaving this meeting, Mr. Hawkins. Not if you ever plan on doing business with us that is," the leader of the three men said. He was a young man in his late twenties, and had long blond hair that was up in a stylish ponytail. He also happened to be the owner of *Mendacium*.

"My son is in the hospital," Hawkins explained, "I have to go. It's an emergency. Can't we reschedule this some other time?" The three men looked at each other, and leaned in to discuss Jeremiah's question. The oldest among them named Morris, lifted his head from the huddle and spoke.

"I am afraid it's today or never, Mr. Hawkins. Let me remind you of how much money you stand to make from this deal. Besides, our meeting will only take another hour or so to finalize everything." The final man of the three now chose to speak as well. He wore a yellow bow-tie, and his face was very white. He had bags under his eyes, and he looked as if he was in very poor health. His voice was wild, with varying pitches and tones that made him sound like a crazy person.

"Mr. Hawkins!" he bellowed. "Surely, your son can wait. Doctors are very melodramatic when it comes to these types of things as I am sure you are well aware of. This will all be over shortly." The man stood up and reached out his hand to shake. "Let's finalize this like men, shall we?"

Jeremiah knew that this merger would mean not millions of dollars for his company, but billions. Maybe the man with the yellow bow-tie was right. What if he showed up at the hospital and the whole thing turned out to be nothing more than just a scare. But this was him rationalizing things like he had always done. He knew by the doctor's tone that this was more than just a few scrapes and bruises. This is the stuff you see on TV, but it's never supposed to happen to people you love. And besides, Joshua was all he had left, after Marcus had ... but there was no point reliving that memory. He knew the decision he had to make.

"I'm sorry, gentlemen; I think my company is just moving in a different direction than yours." The three men's mouths hung open. They were not used to being refused, especially not by someone whose track record was as shady as Jeremiah's.

"You are making a big mistake," said Morris.

"You will regret this decision I assure you," the young blond man added.

"This is bigger than just companies, Hawkins! This is your reputation at stake!" chimed the sickly fellow now withdrawing his hand from the shake position.

"I think my reputation as a business man is nowhere near as tarnished as my reputation as a father. It's time I got my priorities straight. You are welcome to stay, but as for me, I am going to see my son." Jeremiah grabbed his suitcase and coat, and headed out of his office door. The three men calling after him, but their words falling on deaf ears.

"That makes twice in one day that we have been rejected," said Morris.

"We have one last try," said the young man with blond hair, "see that you don't screw it up for us."

The sickly man smiled crazily, as he played with the yellow ring around his finger.

"Don't worry," he said, "I can be very persuasive."

8

A NIGHT IN CARCOSA

J•OSHUA CAME TO THE END of the mountain passage, surprised now to see that it was night outside. He wondered how he could have traveled all day and not have known it. He knew for a fact that he could have only been in the tunnel for maybe six hours. But, he also knew that time was strange here, and stranger still was the way in which nature acted in this place. He emerged to find it not only night, but raining heavily. He didn't mind it, however, because the rain would help clean away the dirt, blood, sap, and bug juices that had accumulated on his body throughout his journey.

The narrow path was now becoming more pronounced. Even having rock outlining in some areas. He assumed that this meant he was getting closer to his destination, wherever that was. There was talk of the Master's kingdom, or His house, so one of those two was probably his final destination. Or, if Hell was Lovelight, maybe the Kingdom was Heaven? But did he really deserve that? In his world he would have said yes. But now, he thought it more and more unlikely that the Master would allow someone like him entrance.

Joshua continued down the path, looking back only once to see the small mountain fading off in the distance. The night was cold, and the rain had now completely soaked Joshua's clothes, causing him to shiver. He decided it would probably be best to make camp, or look for some sort of shelter until the rain blew over.

He wasn't long down the path before he noticed two lit up spires sticking out above the treetops. These were the types of spires that

belonged to old Castles built from time immemorial. The kind that
you would see in old scary movies, with monsters and dungeons
buried deep inside hidden chambers. He ran along the path,
heading for the two spires, as the rest of the castle came into view.
What he saw, however, was not one castle, but two.

In the middle of the narrow path was a tiny gate connected to
a very large fence on either side. The fence was in turn connected
by two enormous castles. On the left side was a sign that read,
"Castle Carcosa," and on the right side was a sign that read, "Castle
Prospero."

Joshua walked up to the tiny gate, and was not surprised to find
that it was locked. He was skilled enough to climb it, but decided
that it would be a bad idea to do so without permission. If he was
caught on the other side by someone from either one of the two
castles, they would regard him as no more than a thief or robber
coming to steal their things. He would attempt the castles first, and
see if he could get permission to proceed.

His first stop was "Castle Prospero". He walked up the stairs
leading to the massive wooden door, only to find it barred shut
with a sign that read, "You are not welcome here death!" He
appreciated their sentiments, but thought it all very odd. The place
also had a foul odor that seemed to seep through the tiny cracks
in the door.

He decided to move on to the next castle in hopes of a friendlier
welcome. He walked across the narrow path, and into the courtyard
of Carcosa. He was moving fairly quickly, not wanting to be far
from the narrow path for long. Upon entering the courtyard, the
rain abruptly stopped, and the sky was suddenly clear and devoid
of clouds. The night was very strange on this side of the path, and
the stars glowed an iridescent black. There were four moons that
moved across the sky, switching positions with one another like
dance partners. Joshua also noticed looking down; that his shadow
in the moonlight would grow and shrink as if it was dancing right
along with the celestial bodies.

The castle itself looked very old. Parapets broken and
crumbling from years of neglect. There were gargoyles lining the

roof, and small streams of water trickled out of their mouths. There were holes the size of cannonballs in some of the top towers, and Joshua imagined that this place must have seen its share of battles throughout the decades. Moss and fungus lined the sides of the walls, and grass burst forth from the cracks in the stone on the ground.

Joshua ran up the stone stairway that lead to the massive door of Carcosa. He found this door unbarred and sign free, and just as he had reached the final step, the door came swinging open. Standing before him was an eight foot tall man who had to weigh less than ninety-pounds. His tuxedo clung to his body and was three sizes too small. It was so tight fitting that the man sported a midriff.

"The King has been expecting you," the man said in a very Lurch like manner. "Please, follow me."

Joshua, not wanting to offend the owner of the castle, followed after the man, the door shutting behind them. The interior of the castle was tenebrous and dusty. Cobwebs hung from the chandelier perched high above the main chamber. Aligning the walls were hundreds of paintings reaching all the way up to the ceiling.

"Just this way," the tall-butler said, noticing that Joshua had stopped walking and was now gawking at his new surroundings.

"Sorry," replied Joshua, "I love art." Meaning this to be a compliment, but coming out as presumptuous. The butler stared at him with his stoic-constantly-frowning face, and motioned for Joshua to continue.

The two men walked through a small door that was just to the right of a large staircase centered in the middle of the main entrance hall. The door opened up into a very long hallway with doors along the sides. These doors all had plaques on them with various names. One read, "Dr. Mengele's Office," another, "Mr. Jones Office." There had to be at least fifteen doors on either side of the hallway, each one with a different plaque with a different name on it.

Joshua followed after the skinny-butler, almost having to run to keep up with his long strides. Each one of his strides took Joshua three steps just to keep pace. The butler made an abrupt turn to the left, and was once more down another long hallway.

"Keep up," the butler grunted, as he took up an even faster pace. Joshua was in full gallop now and fast on the man's heels as they took turn after turn into a seemingly endless labyrinth of hallways and doors. It wasn't until he passed the hallway with all the office doors once again that he realized something was amiss. Before he could say anything, however, they stepped through the door at the end of the hallway and suddenly found themselves in a large room with a throne at the far end.

The butler stopped abruptly, and Joshua, being unable to halt his body's momentum, came crashing into the back of the lanky-man sending both men crashing to the ground. The two men scrambled to their feet, as the sound of a loud bang came from the end of the throne room. Joshua looked for the source of the sound, and found that one of the floor panels next to the throne had been thrown open. This was a sort of escape hatch, or perhaps a secret underground room he imagined. Whatever it was, someone, or something was coming out of it, and Joshua felt a chill run down his spine as its occupant emerged.

A tall slender man wearing a pallid mask walked slowly up the underground staircase leading into the throne room. He wore a long tattered yellow robe with two very large red wings made from the feathers of various creatures sewn into the shoulders. The robe was long, and trailed a few feet behind the man. The tips of the red wings drug across the floor behind the man as he bent down and closed up the floor hatch.

"Wonderful, wonderful! My guest has finally arrived!" the man said, clapping his hands, as the butler scurried off to attend to other matters. "I hope that your journey here was not very taxing?"

"I'm sorry, you were expecting me? But I don't even know who you are," Joshua said confused.

"You may call me the Yellow King of course! Everyone does, although some prefer to call me by other names in order to avoid associations with a business man such as myself. These hipsters now of days! Am I right?"

"You're a King?" Joshua asked unconvinced. "Then surely you must know of the One whose Kingdom is just beyond your gate outside. I assume it is your gate, yes?"

"Of course it is my gate! What do you think? It's attached to my place of business just for giggles? And yes Mr. Smarty-pants, I am a king! Don't all kings have castles? How young are you not to know basic principles such as these?" The Yellow King asked rather indignantly.

"I apologize, I did not mean to offend you," Joshua said apologetically. "And not to push the matter further, but you didn't answer everything. Do you know about the Kingdom that lies just beyond your gate? Do you know of its owner?"

"Of course I know who lives there! Everyone in these parts knows about Him. You could even say that I am one of His biggest fans! Have you ever read His book? Not to brag, but I could quote the entire thing if you so wished," the Yellow king said proudly.

"Then I guess my next question is, may I have your permission to use the gate outside?"

The Yellow King glided across the room pacing back and forth, mulling Joshua's request over. He hovered over to the throne and sat down popping his knuckles as he stared at Joshua with his intense eyes. These were dark yellow eyes that contrasted the pale white mask, making them look like two yellow gems faceted into the mask.

Suddenly, and without warning, the Yellow King burst into tears, banging his fists against the armrests of the throne as he did. Joshua, not knowing what to do or say, just stood there taken aback by the entire ordeal.

"Why would you want to leave? What have I done, Joshua? What have I done to deserve such impolite behavior from you? Is it because I don't call enough? Is it my weight? Because I can lose more if it will make you love me! Just tell me what to do, and I'll do it!" The Yellow King shrieked as he started to unintelligibly wail.

"I don't know what I said, sir. If I offended you then I ..." Joshua stammered out these words but was quickly interrupted by the sound of laughter.

"And the Academy Award goes to …" The Yellow King slapped his hands against his armchair making a drum-roll. "The Yellow King for best performance of all time in a throne room!" The Yellow King started clapping as he ran around the room pretending to high-five invisible members of an audience. He jumped up on a table that was in the far corner and started giving a speech.

"I really want to thank Joshua here for being a wonderful supporting actor. Without his continued dedication, I wouldn't be where I am today! Oh great, I see the little light flashing red. They never give us enough time up here! Well, thank you all and goodnight!" The Yellow King jumped off the table, and ran out a back door hidden behind the throne. Joshua, completely clueless as to what he just witnessed, stood in disbelief.

A few seconds later the door behind the throne burst open, and the Yellow King came gliding in.

"Now, where were we?" the Yellow King asked. "Oh yes, the gate outside! First, let me show you around the place and give you a little insight into what I do for a living, sound good?"

"What was that all about just then?" Joshua demanded. "And how do you know my name?"

"Wonderful! Shall we start our tour of the castle then? After the tour, you can be on your way," the King explained.

"So you will unlock the gate then?" Joshua asked once more.

"Right this way, Joshua. I am a very busy man you see. Not many people are privy to the inner workings of this place. You should feel honored young man! And the whole business of the gate we will discuss after. Now, please keep your hands inside the vehicle at all times while the ride is in progress."

The King grabbed Joshua by the arm, and he was immediately whisked off into the endless hallways of the castle. He tried to free himself, but the King had a vice-like grip on his arm and was incredibly powerful for his size.

"On your right and left, you will see the offices of our employees. These are men and women that I have worked with throughout the years. They are all perfectly brilliant if I do say so

myself, and it's all thanks to my inspiration! Shall we continue?"
The King asked this last question as if Joshua had any say in the
matter. Before he knew it, he was dragged off down another
hallway and led into a large dining room with hundreds of paintings
all hanging askew across the walls.

"These are some of the pieces I have collected over the years,
all of which I have inspired in some fashion, though the artists
would never mention my name of course. I never mind though.
Maybe I'm too modest. What do you think?" The King said, as he
pointed out various paintings mounted on the wall.

"Are you a fan of Albrecht Dürer? Of course you are, who isn't?
Well here is one of my favorites of his."

Joshua gazed up and saw a painting of a Knight on a horse.
This was all he could make out, however, for he was soon hurried
along the wall to another painting.

"This one is entitled *Benois Madonna*," the King said, pointing
up to a large painting of a woman holding a very plump child. "It's
one of my favorites! Isn't that baby precious? Maybe if you were
home more we could have one of our own! Anyways, paintings in
this vein have helped business grow exponentially. Last few are a
set, and then we move on." Joshua's arm is yanked hard, and he is
dragged to the very end of the wall. In front of him is a series of
eight paintings, all telling a story.

"This set is called *A Rake's Progress.* True story oddly enough.
Saw the whole thing play out with my very eyes, then I told old
Hogarth about it, and what does he do? He goes and makes a
painting of it, taking all the credit of course. But that's usually how
all my clients work. Doesn't matter though, my business booms
off their success! Let's continue, shall we? These paintings depress
me," the Yellow King said, laughing hysterically as he led Joshua
wildly down another hallway.

"How much longer?" Joshua asked. "I really must be on my
way."

"Oh darling, you mustn't go!" The King said in a Humphrey
Bogart type voice. "The night is young and so are we!"

The two men descended, and then immediately ascended a set of stairs before arriving in a large circular library. There were metal winding staircases leading up to the multiple floors. Joshua counted thirty-six floors before losing sight and giving up count.

"Look at our collection of literature! All of which I co-authored by the way," the King said, winking at Joshua.

"On the first floor we have non-fiction. Well, that's not entirely true. All of our floors are non-fiction. We have such titles as *The Urantia Book, Poem of the Man God, The Holy Blood and the Holy Grail, The Communist Manifesto, Mein Kampf,* and so many others that I can't even remember them all! And to think, I had a hand in writing all of these. All best sellers might I add," the King boasted—something he was very fond of doing.

"But I know about a lot of these books. I have even read a few of them," Joshua said as he picked up an ancient copy of Hamlet that looked as if it was an original. "You didn't write any of these."

"Inspired my boy, inspired. I myself cannot create; I can only adapt that which has already been created. The King beyond that fence is the One who creates. Myself, and a few other like-minded individuals persuade and coerce the created into doing what we want. Sometimes we get entire novels filled with our propaganda. Other times, we get only snippets of our message portrayed. Either way, no publicity is bad publicity am I right?" The King explained.

"You work with Lanirche, don't you?" Joshua asked.

"We are acquaintances yes. My approach is much more subtle than his, however. But come, we have talked long enough in here. There is still one last part of the castle I would like to show you before I eat you. Just kidding of course! Or am I? Oh, I crack myself up!"

Joshua tried even harder to escape the Yellow King's grasp, but the King seemed entirely unfazed by his effort. The two men rushed out the door of the dining room and into another long corridor. They swished around the corner and through a large doorway leading into a colossal amphitheater. Joshua had no idea how the castle that he had seen outside was housing such rooms as these. It was as if the castle was a separate dimension or universe with endless possibilities for rooms.

"Oh, now, this is lovely isn't it? A little gaudy for my taste, but it will do for our performance. Quick, let's have a seat, the show is about to begin!"

The Yellow King led Joshua unwillingly to the front row of the theater. The two men sat down as the King pulled out a box of chocolate candies with a mint center.

"Want some?" He asked Joshua, shaking the box in front of him. Joshua stared back in bewilderment.

"Fine, more for me," the King said. "And Joshua, will you please be quiet! The play is about to start! Sorry about that sir, he won't say another word," the King explained to an empty seat behind him.

The lights of the theater went out, and the stage-lights came up full blast. Onstage was the set of an old courtroom from the 17th century. Actors emerged from the wings, all looking identical to the butler who had answered the door of the castle.

"You are a witch," said one of the lanky-men dressed as a judge.

"No I am not," said another, this one in a dress, complete with bonnet.

"Kill her," said the lanky-judge.

"Yes, we will," answered a few others onstage in colonial attire.

The curtain lowered, and the King stood up applauding madly.

"Bravo! Bravo! Encore!" The King shouted pulling out a handkerchief and blowing his nose into it.

"Almost brings tears to your eyes doesn't it?" he asked.

"Not really," Joshua replied, "why would it?"

"Some people just don't appreciate fine art!" the King said with a sigh, turning once more to the empty chair behind him.

"Sir, would you please remove your feet from the back of my chair? Can you believe this guy, Joshy? Can I call you Joshy? Shhhhh, the next act is starting!" The King said shushing Joshua who wasn't even talking.

The curtain lifted, and a backdrop of an outdoor battle was lowered into place. The same tall lanky-men came out, this time dressed in armor, with two of them wearing robes and female wigs.

"You are in our land," the lanky-armored men said to the two cross-dressing men.

"Please, don't hurt us," the lanky-women actors pleaded.

"It is for the church," said the lanky-knights, as they walked slowly over to the women and ran them through with their swords. The curtain closed once more before lifting for the actors to take a bow. The Yellow King stood up clapping frantically and whistling with his fingers in his mouth.

"More of the same! More of the same!" he shouted, as the curtain came slamming to the stage floor.

"Can you believe that, Joshy? What a performance! I was on the edge of my seat the entire time! And that part with the swords! Just ... wow."

"It was alright I guess. Now I really must be going sir. I have to get to the Master's Kingdom. I am on a journey," Joshua explained.

"You travelers and your 'journeys'," the King said mockingly. "Joshua, I have inspired so many men and women; inspired them to greatness. I showed you all of this because everyone wants to be remembered. I can make that happen for you. You could have an entire shelf of books in my library with your name on them. Perhaps an entire wall with your artwork? An event that will never be forgotten? You name it; I can give you the tools to make it happen. I have been giving you small ideas all of your life whether you knew it or not," the King continued.

"I have an associate, Mr. Wilde; he can repair things that have been tarnished. Perhaps you have a past you would like to forget about? I can give you his card. What do you say Joshua?" the King asked, reaching into his pocket and pulling out a yellow seal.

"I want to give you this seal, it's my calling card. Anyone who wears it is protected by the Yellow King. You would be surprised at how many people wear my emblem if you just opened your eyes and looked! So, what do you say? Be my valentine?" he asked, holding out the yellow seal and fluttering his eyelids.

Joshua had wanted to be remembered all his life. He stood in his brother's shadow in college, and now, he was vice-president of his father's company. He could never make a name for himself in his world, not with his upbringing. Everyone would always assume that everything was handed to him on a silver platter. The King's offer was indeed tempting. Isn't that what everyone wants in life? To be remembered?

"And what do I have to give up if I take this seal?" Joshua asked. "I refuse to have any business with Lanirche as well, so if we do this, he has no part in it."

"I think Lanirche could be persuaded to stay out of this little transaction of ours. As far as what you give up, I simply ask that you rid yourself of that asphyxiating Spirit that has been following you around this entire time. I do hate it when He comes into the house. I start coughing all over the place, and his incessant groaning goes on-and-on about all matter of things. He has to go, and then everything can be yours."

"What are you talking about?" Joshua asked. "What Spirit?"

"Yowza, yowza, yowza!" the Yellow King said slapping his knee. "You are further along than I thought! Already completely ignoring the Spirit! That usually comes after years of following the Master's rules. I must say, I'm impressed. Whoever was assigned to you in your world has done a wonderful job of keeping you blind to certain things. I will have to send them a bonus check this Halloween!"

"Apostolos did mention a Spirit I think. Did he? No, he did. I remember it now ..." Joshua said quietly to himself, as the Yellow King ran around looking for some parchment to write on.

"Ah, forget it," the King said, giving up his search. "I'll just make a mental note to do it. Now, He must go. I can barely breathe in here!" The King exclaimed, pulling out an inhaler from deep within his robes. An un-see-able mist began to pervade the room, and Joshua finally understood what it was that the King was talking about.

It wasn't so much with sight, but with feeling that Joshua realized it. A breeze that hit Joshua like a ton of bricks, and penetrated his entire body, filling him with a power that was like no other. Joshua felt strong, but more than that, he felt wise. Everything he had seen and heard came rushing to his mind. The chains, Apostolos, Lovelight, the Ghost Tree; everything. He had been tempted before, but this time he felt the temptation. He felt the words of the King like one would feel a sickness. The words were foreign to his body, and he would having nothing to do with them; not now, not ever.

Power, fame, women, money, drugs, stuff, stuff, and more stuff. Was this as far as Lanirche and his flunkies could go? They could offer earthly things and nothing else. They could offer years of happiness, but not an eternity of happiness. Joshua was seeing things through a new lens, and whatever this Spirit was that the King was talking about, was his window into this new understanding.

"What happens in my world doesn't really matter much I think," Joshua said with a strange authority. "I think I am meant to just pass through that place. Besides, if I ever return, I will delight in the shade of other people's shadows from now on. I am tired of trying to make a name for myself. Tired of looking up to people who are just like me; flawed. I have a path now, a purpose. Something far beyond anything you could offer me," he continued.

"Now, if you would be so kind as to take off your mask, sir. I laid aside my disguise many hours ago," Joshua said, not certain why he said it, but knowing it was the right thing to say.

"Of course! Lost another one!" The King shouted stomping his feet in a tantrum. "How is it fair when we don't know which ones are His children? It's all a gamble man, and He's playing with loaded dice!" The King exclaimed throwing his arms in the air.

"Take off your mask!" Joshua repeated this time yelling.

"Mask? I wear no mask!" The King shouted back in defeat, pocketing his yellow seal.

"Be on your way!" The King sneered. "Your ethereal friend's groaning is going to wake the neighbors! I have a business to run here! It's unprofessional with him gliding around!"

"So you will unlock the gate then?" Joshua asked.

"Please, I never had the key in the first place. That gate only unlocks to those whom your Friend there allows. Now be gone, before someone drops a house on you!" the King said as he skipped away, lifting his long yellow tattered robes and singing loudly to himself. Joshua opened the first door he could find, eager to be rid of Castle Carcosa and its lunatic King. He found upon opening the door, that he was immediately back outside in Carcosa's courtyard. As he stepped back onto the narrow path, the night faded and in seconds the light of morning had returned as the tiny gate at the end of the path clicked open.

9
Get Cleaned Up

J OSHUA WAS RELIEVED TO FIND HIS OLD FRIEND Apostolos waiting just on the other side of the tiny gate.

"My friend," said Apostolos, "how happy I am to see you after all this time!" Joshua stepped through the gate, and was welcomed into the Master's Kingdom with a hug from his friend. He was welcomed not as a guest, thief, or stranger; but as a fellow citizen. This was his home now, this was where his name would be made great. This was where all of the trials he had overcome would be celebrated, and where all of his mistakes would be remembered no more.

"We have been celebrating all day because of you, Joshua! There have been songs and feasts and much dancing, for once you were dead, but now you have been made alive!" Apostolos whispered all these things into Joshua's ear, and he felt his neck become wet with Apostolos' tears. Joshua also began to cry as the two men embraced. They pulled apart and looked at each other, both men laughing as they wiped their faces.

"Apostolos, I have so many questions about so many things! I feel so light, and yet so burdened. I feel like for once in my life I can truly understand things. I was talking with the Yellow King, and all at once he demanded that I be rid of something that I could not see. I didn't understand what he was talking about, and yet, I completely understood. It was as if he was asking me to cut myself in half. To separate something that has always been with me, but I just never understood what it was."

"The 'Spirit', he called it. Anyways, at that moment I felt something hit me. Like a sucker punch out of nowhere, I was sight-sided. I could see the King for what he truly was. He wore a mask that hid who he really was, but I saw that the mask was really not a mask at all, but his true face. He is a deceiver, and he masquerades about drawing others into his madness. But I knew, Apostolos; I knew in that instant that he was temporary. That what he was offering was temporary, and that his kingdom was fleeting. I also knew that he held no authority over me, and that I belonged to another."

Joshua finished taking a deep breath.

"That man has been causing trouble for thousands of years, and most men go all of their lives without recognizing what only took you a matter of minutes. But as you said, his days are numbered. One day we shall storm his dreaded Castle, and his insanity will be tolerated no more." Apostolos said, grabbing Joshua around the shoulder and guiding him down the narrow path.

"But what of this Spirit?" Joshua asked. "What exactly does it do?"

"For me to answer that fully would be impossible. That you must work out for yourself with fear and trembling. I will tell you this though. He is a far greater guide than an infinite number of me's put together. Listen to Him, Joshua. He will show you what is required as a citizen in the Master's Kingdom," Apostolos explained.

"I guess I can live with that answer," Joshua replied. "One last question, if you don't mind though."

"I will do my best to answer it," said Apostolos.

"How much further on this road before I am done," Joshua asked. "I am tired, Apostolos. I am so very tired."

"You will not continue the path in this place, my friend," Apostolos explained. "You must take up the road in your world, and help others along as well. You know the journey, now you must guide others just as I have guided you. You will return to your body Joshua, for you are not dead, but have only been sleeping."

"But how will I know what to say to others? I barely understand any of this myself! Can't you come with me?" Joshua pleaded.

"There are many like me in your world that will help you along the path. Do you really think you are the only person to walk this road? To be tempted and tried as you have? You are one of a multitude, but you must persevere just as they have before you," Apostolos explained, lifting up the sleeve of his robe. On his wrist, Joshua was surprised to see a watch.

"Enough questions. All will be revealed in its proper time. Now, if you are to return to your body and to your world, there is only one order of business left. We must hurry as well, because there is very little time to complete our final task."

"Final task?" Joshua asked confused. "What is there left to do?"

"Look at yourself, Joshua! You are a mess!" Apostolos said picking at Joshua's filthy collar. It was true, he was a mess. He was covered in bug juice, blood, tree sap, dirt, sweat, and many other unknown things that were only resident to this land.

"It's time you got cleaned up," said Apostolos. "Now quickly, follow me. I may be old, but in this place I can run like a gazelle."

Apostolos leaped into the air as if weightless and headed down the narrow path with Joshua in hot pursuit. The two men were barely touching the ground, as if gravity didn't really apply in this place. The path in front of them cut straight through a mountain, but instead of being another cave, this was a clear cut ravine. Off on the horizon, just between the two rocky sides of the path, Joshua could see the most beautiful city imaginable.

It's buildings were crystal clear and were beyond any architectural feats ever created by man. In the middle of the city was a giant castle that looked as if it was made of pure light. As if light itself was being held together to form a solid mass. He noticed that there was no sun in the sky as he gazed at the city, for the castle itself gave off so much light, that the sun was no longer needed.

"Apostolos!" Joshua called ahead. "Is that what I think it is?"

"It is so much more than what you are thinking, Joshua! So much more than any of us ever thought!" Apostolos called back.

The two men continued at breakneck speeds, until Joshua noticed Apostolos slowing his pace.

"Just ahead, Joshua!" Apostolos called back. "Stop up here!" he said, pointing to his left.

The rock on either side of the path began to expand outward, forming a large opening. To the left of the path was a small pool that reminded Joshua of a hot spring by the way it bubbled. At the end of the path was yet another gate, this one, however, was very large, ivory white in color, and imposing.

"Here we are," Apostolos said as they arrived at the pool. "This will feel like nothing you have ever felt before, and after it's over, you will never be the same." The two men stepped into the tiny pool of water which immediately stopped bubbling upon them entering. The water became completely still, and to Joshua it felt as if it was seeping through his pores and into his blood. His body told him to jump out and run. To escape this solvent that penetrated not only the outside, but the inside.

"Are you ready, brother?" Apostolos asked.

"I am ready Apostolos," Joshua said smiling, "Clean me up."

10
VISIBLE SIGNS, INVISIBLE REALITIES

HOSPITAL WAITING ROOM IN CHICAGO/A tiny pool in another world ...

"Doctor Gonzalez, we need you now!"

The nurse's voice had a nervous quiver as she rushed into the waiting room where Dr. Gonzalez was speaking with Mr. Hawkins and his two wives. The doctor had heard this same quiver before and knew it never meant anything good for the patient.

"Nurse, stay with the Hawkins'." Doctor Gonzalez quickly washed his hands, and pulled on new latex gloves as he ran down the hallway and jumped into action.

"Is he going to be alright?" asked Katrina Hawkins (Joshua's step-mother).

"Yes, is *MY* boy going to be ok?" asked Elizabeth Hawkins.

"Dr. Gonzalez is the best we have, if anyone can help your son, it's him," the nurse replied, attempting to calm the two mothers. Jeremiah Hawkins walked over to one of the chairs in the waiting room. He sat down, breathing in deeply, taking in the smell of antiseptics. He had sat in this same chair twice before, once for the birth of his son Marcus and the other for the birth of Joshua.

"Congratulations, Mr. Hawkins! You are a father!" the Nurse had said all those years ago. He remembered that first feeling of holding his child. Looking into his son's eyes and seeing himself, seeing something that he had helped create. But what had he done now? He had created a business, and it had become his child. But it couldn't call him father, it couldn't love him. He had thrown away years of memories with his children, and for what? A nice house that he never slept in? A car that he never drove? A failed marriage, and two dead sons? He had gained the world, but lost his soul.

"I don't know if you can hear me," Jeremiah whispered, "but please, if you are real, save my only son." He covered his face in his hands and wept. His two wives sitting down on either side of him, doing the same.

Doctor Gonzalez came bursting through the door of the ICU as Joshua is rushed into emergency surgery. All the while, the droning beep of Joshua's EKG declared that the heart to which it is attached, had stopped. He called for one of the nurses to grab the defibrillator, and slid his hands around both handles.

"He's gone," said a man in a white doctor's robe, placing his arm on Gonzalez's shoulder.

"Please," said Gonzalez, "this will work. I know it."

He placed the plates strategically on Joshua's chest and …

Apostolos grabbed Joshua's hand and the back of his head and leaned him backwards into the small pool …

"Clear!" Doctor Gonzalez yelled …

Apostolos dunked Joshua under the water,
"In the name of the Father," he said.
 Emerging, Joshua's eyes began to blur …

"Nothing sir …" the nurse said sorrowfully.
"Ok, increasing voltage then. Clear!" Gonzalez rubbed the plates together, and again placed them upon Joshua's chest …

A second time Joshua is dunked by Apostolos.
"And of the Son."
Joshua's eyes start to go black as he comes out a second time…

"Nothing Doctor … no response. Call it now!" argued the other doctor.

"No, please, once more. Clear!" With desperation, Gonzalez pressed down hard as electricity coursed through Joshua's chest …

Joshua's world began to phase out in static. The last thing he noticed before his mind went blank was the water around him turning black and red while his clothes became bleach white.

"And of the Holy Spirit," Apostolos finished. His hands now empty, and the body of Joshua gone from that world …

Joshua's body jerked on the table as his heart monitor jolted back to a steady beep. His body took a deep breath and then remained still. At the same time, the doctors and nurses all took a deep breath as well.

"Well done, Doctor. You were right," said the other doctor feeling ashamed. Meanwhile, the nurses checked vitals and fluids to make sure Joshua was fully stabilized.

"I guess the Big Man upstairs was on our side today," Gonzalez said. "Sometimes the good guys win."

Gonzalez took his gloves off and headed towards the waiting room where two crying mothers were waiting to hold their baby boy.

11
FIN

FEW DAYS PASSED BEFORE JOSHUA finally came back to consciousness. During those days, the swelling in his brain went down considerably, and they took him off the drugs that put him in his comatose state. His brain functions returned to normal, and the bullet wounds in his chest were starting to heal miraculously well. Both of his mothers took shifts at his bedside, while his father did most of his business work via his laptop in the waiting room, leaving his special chair only to grab food and use the restroom.

"Wouldn't you be more comfortable sleeping in your bed at home, Sweetie?" his new wife Katrina asked.

"I'll only leave when Joshua himself tells me to," he replied.

Joshua would mutter things here and there about a man named Apostolos, and about following some strange path.

"Lanirche!" He cried late one night, as his step-mom rubbed his sweating forehead with a rag.

It was like this off and on for quite some time, until one fateful Sunday, Joshua opened his eyes. His vision was blurred, and at first he thought he saw Metatron standing over him, but it was just a nurse checking his fluids. She didn't notice that he had opened his eyes, until Joshua reached out and grabbed her sleeve. The nurse let out a small scream, grabbing her chest as she jumped backwards.

"My heavens! You almost scared me to death young man!" she said half smiling, half laughing. "Glad to see you awake. We have been watching you like a hawk." The nurse checked his monitors, and then pressed a button next to his bed.

"Where … where am I?" Joshua asked groggily.

"You are in the hospital, young man. You have been through quite an ordeal. I just called for your doctor. Your mothers and father are here as well. They will be in shortly."

The elderly nurse leaned over the hospital bed, strapped a band around Joshua's arm, and checked his blood pressure.

"I'm sorry, did you say my parents are here? Did you say my father?" Joshua asked skeptically.

"Of course they are! Your father has been here ever since you first arrived. He has refused to leave in fact," the nurse replied.

"After they see you, we have a few tests we will have to run to make sure you are recovering as planned. Then, you will have to talk with the police once you're feeling up to it. You have been comatose for about three weeks now, and they would like to know exactly what happened in that alleyway," she explained.

Joshua tried to sit up, but was suddenly knocked back down by the pain in his chest. His head was throbbing, and reaching up his hands, he felt his head wrapped in bandages.

"What happened to me?" Joshua asked.

"You were shot while saving a young girl's life, Joshua. The bullets weren't the problem though, you smacked your head on the pavement and fractured the back of your skull. I am sure it will all come back to you in the next few days," the nurse said reassuringly, as a knock came to the door.

"Come in!" the nurse yelled.

Joshua's mother came walking in followed by his father and step-mother, tears streaming down their faces.

"Joshy!" His mother cried falling on top of him, and squeezing him as tight as she could.

"Mom! Please, my chest!" He shrieked in pain.

"Oh, sweetie! I love you, please know that. I love you, I am sorry for everything! Sorry for being a bad mother and for—"

"Mom, Mom, please, It's all okay. I know you love me. Do you know I love you?" Joshua asked, kissing his mother's cheek.

"Katrina," Joshua called to his stepmother, "thank you for being here. I remember hearing your voice while I was asleep. Thank you, and I love you as well."

His stepmother burst into tears, and made a little wave as she blew a kiss to her stepson.

"Hey Dad," Joshua said, "good to see you, sir."

Jeremiah Hawkins walked slowly over to his sons bed, and knelt down grabbing his hand in his.

"On the ride over here Joshua, I thought … I thought I had lost you. I thought I would never get to tell you how proud I am of you. You know, I never told Marcus how … and well. And then, these last few days of waiting, not knowing if we would get woken in the middle of the night. It's just that, well … I'm sorry I haven't always been there. I thought I was doing the right thing in raising you. I was afraid to get close after what happened with your brother, and I never had much of a father and–" Jeremiah was interrupted mid-sentence by Joshua who held his father's hand for the first time in his entire life.

His father's hand felt so big in his, and he realized that no matter how old he got, he would always feel small around his dad. It was just the way that sons were supposed to feel.

"I know Dad," Joshua said. "No need for apologies. I haven't been the son to you and Mom that I should be either. That is all behind us now. I have so much to tell both of–"

This time, Joshua was interrupted by Doctor Gonzalez who entered with a large grin upon his face.

"Well, how about this! The whole family's here! No need to get up, Joshua. It's not like I saved your life or anything," Gonzalez said winking, reaching out his hand to shake Joshua's. Joshua lifted his hand as high as he could, and Gonzalez leaned down to meet his grasp.

"You had us all scared for a while! You really should learn to dodge bullets if you're going to be running around saving people's lives!" He said laughing, as he checked Joshua's chart making a few marks with his pen.

"All joking aside, you should get some rest. There will be plenty of time for talking later," Gonzalez explained.

Joshua and his parents exchanged many more snot mixed-with-saliva kisses before saying their goodbyes.

"I'll be taking the next few weeks off to make sure you have a smooth recovery, Son," Jeremiah said patting Joshua's arm.

"No need for that Dad. I'll be out of here in no time. I would like to talk with you about some things though, about the business and what not," said Joshua.

"Of course, Son. I have some things to tell you about that as well. Plenty of time for that later though. Get some sleep. Your mother ... mothers and I will be here if you need anything." Jeremiah hurried Joshua's mothers out of the room, and within seconds Joshua was fast asleep.

A week later and Joshua is still in the hospital but recovering well. Officer Hunneh calls ahead to make sure Joshua is feeling well enough to answer some questions, and arrives soon after getting the go ahead. He slides past a nurse exiting the room and gives an awkward apology as the two get jammed in the narrow doorway together. Joshua chuckles under his breath as the nurse leaves, and Officer Hunneh gives a small laugh as well.

"Mr. Hawkins, I am Officer Caleb Hunneh. I was the first officer to arrive on the scene. I need to ask you just a few questions to finish my police report. That is, if you are feeling up to it of course."

Caleb pulled up a chair and sat down next to Joshua, who turned off the television.

"I am glad to see you're up and talking after everything you have been through," Caleb remarked. "I'll be honest; I thought all three of you were goners. You're one lucky son of a–"

"Luck had nothing to do with it, Officer," Joshua corrected. "Blessed maybe? I'll go with that. What questions did you have for me? I'll be honest, I don't remember much. It all happened so fast."

"Well, the first question would be: What led you down that alleyway?" Caleb asked.

Joshua took a sip of his awful sugary-water-drink, and thought for a second.

"I heard a scream, and then I remember running. I saw a man attacking a woman, and my body kind of took over from there. I started wrestling with the mugger, and then I remember another man. About the time I saw the other guy though, I had already hit pavement, so I can't really describe what he looked like," Joshua said apologetically.

"That other man that ran in there saved your life. We have an eyewitness who called 911 that saw the whole thing. If he had not run in when he did, the mugger would have probably put a bullet right between your eyes," Caleb explained.

Joshua sat in disbelief. He had no idea that in his attempt to save that girl's life, he had actually had his own life saved as well.

"What was the man's name? Or, can I not know that?" Joshua asked.

"The man who saved your life is one Walter Sparks," Caleb answered. "From our eyewitness account, we know that he ran in to help, and was shot in the head during the struggle. The muggers own gun went off twice during the fight and he ended up shooting himself as well. We found all three of you bleeding out on the pavement. The mugger died in the hospital days later despite all signs that he would be okay. His heart just stopped for some reason. He got what he deserved if you ask me though. The other guy, Walter, died within seconds of being shot by the coroner's estimates. So at least he didn't suffer."

"And the girl? How is she?" Joshua asked.

"She is shaken up of course, but she is okay. She strayed from the main sidewalk, and was trying to take a shortcut. If you hadn't arrived Joshua, she would've been killed. I will be honest with you, this whole thing is a wonder. I am just glad two of you came out alive. Two out of four and two are the good guys." Officer Caleb got up from his chair, and reached out to shake Joshua's hand. "That's really all I needed to know, Joshua. Thanks, and I hope you make a full recovery very soon."

Officer Hunneh slid out of the door, and closed it shut behind him. Joshua let his head fall back, thinking about his conversation with Hunneh as he closed his eyes.

"Walter, where do I know that name? Walter Sparks?" Joshua wracked his brain to remember. His mind wondered a bit, as the name Walter floated around in his brain.

"Walter, Walter, Walter." He repeated the name aloud as he loosened his body, trying to remember. The image of clouds comes to him, and he imagines himself floating through the air. He is a bird soaring through the sky. He swoops and dives and lifts through the air. He catches wind currents and waves at other birds as he soars. Then, he sees it. Something big is coming towards him in the distance. He flaps at high speed, and moves closer to the large object. He is flying past a plane, looking into the windows at the passengers who all looked back out in disgust. Some close their windows, while others just turn away. Apparently, bird-men are frowned upon in this dream.

He flies past a few more windows, and then suddenly he sees a familiar face. He swoops in close, realizing that the face he sees is his own. Sitting next to him on the plane, is another familiar face. It is the face of the man who sat by him before and told him all about the Bible. It is the face of Walter, Walter Sparks. The man who had saved not only his life, but his soul.

AFTERWORD

MY BEST FRIEND ON THIS PLANET has a diet plan that I would like to share with you. Others have resorted to counting calories or working out, but not him; he is an innovator. His method is not very complex. In fact, it's very simple: Stop eating junk. He doesn't eat cake, cookies, candy, pie, or even cakookandie (that's everything listed combined into a shake mixture). He also sticks to drinking water and water only. Guess what; the diet works. He has already lost a ton (literally a ton) of weight without working out or counting calories or any of that other stuff that crazy people do.

Now, some have said, "it's not deprivation, its moderation." He would say those people just aren't strong enough to follow his method. I will be honest; I am not strong enough to do this. I love the occasional soda. I love junk food way too much. Thus, I work out, I count calories, and I try to moderate my junk food intake.

Why do I mention this you may be asking yourself? What does any of this have to do with the story I just read? Well, I am glad you asked. We all have a junk food problem regardless of what you may think. Even my best friend has a junk food problem. The junk I am talking about is the stuff on TV that we feed our minds with. It's the words we say, the books we read, the news we listen to, the shows we watch, the movies we buy, and the music we sing along with. Most of this is junk we put into our bodies, and yet as Christians we say, "Moderation, not deprivation!"

We have a serious sin problem, and even though we try to cut down, and watch our sinful calories, we still consume, consume, consume. When my buddy is asked why he doesn't have a cookie every now and then he always replies with, "You have to get the taste out of your mouth." For him it's a big deal to not eat that junk food because it puts the taste back in your mouth. After a few months of not eating junk, he forgets what that stuff tastes like. He no longer craves it as much as he used to. Sure, he is still tempted every now and then, but it's not as hard.

If we as Christians just stopped consuming all the crap that we do, maybe we could become like this. If we get the taste out of our mouths, in time we will forget what it tasted like. Will we still be tempted? Of course. Does this cutting off require prayer and the Holy Spirit? Is the Pope Catholic? But the first step is admitting you have a problem. Hi, my name is Heath and I have a sin problem. I love the taste of it, but I hate the way it makes me feel. It's the same when you eat too much junk, you have a stomach ache. With sin, I get a heart ache.

I am reminded of one of my favorite books, "The Picture of Dorian Gray". If I could crawl up into the attic of my soul and look at my portrait, I would see a really fat hideous guy staring back at me. Christians and non-Christians alike would see the same thing. Just because Christians are saved doesn't mean their pictures are healthier than non-believers; far from it. We just know that the Master Artist paints us a new picture that never ages.

We all have the sin problem and we all need a Savior. Joshua fed his desires on earth. He stuffed his face with everything he could get his hands on. He needed his spiritual stomach pumped just like all of us do. My prayer is that whoever reads this book will seriously examine their life. Climb up in your attic and look at your painting. Stop the idea of moderation, and try a little sin starvation. Lose the taste my brothers and sisters. Start small and go big. God can do all things, and you have to believe that no sin is too great for Him to forgive.

Thanks for reading my book. I hope you enjoyed at least some of it. If you found it cheesy at times; I'm sorry. Some analogies have to be cheesy to get the point across. If you have any questions about the book, life, love, God, or anything else, please feel free to email me at Corneroftruth@yahoo.com. No spam please, unless it is the delicious canned meat. In that case, send it by the truckload. :)

APPENDIX

Appendix of really hard words and stuff that you were like, "What does that word even mean? I think he made it up. Hey Malcolm, get that dictionary out of the attic and lets nail this little punk on his stupid made up words."

A

Absalom: David's third son in the Bible. He betrayed his father and tried to take over the kingdom. Later, he was speared to a tree by Joab. Epic.

Abyss, The: Refers to a bottomless pit, the underworld, or to Hell. Not a cool place.

Agnostos Theos: The Unknown God. Theorized by some to have been a literal statue that was placed in ancient Greek temples. This is mentioned by Paul in Acts 17:23.

Albrecht Dürer: A German painter who is famous for such works as *Melencolia i*, *Knight, Death and the Devil*, and *Saint Jerome in His Study*. Besides being an awesome painter, he was also a mathematician, a theorist, and a scuba diver.

Akeldama: Means field of blood. This is the field where Judas exploded. Acts 1:18.

Anomie: A term meaning "without law" to describe the lack of social norms. Batman hates Anomie.

Apostolos: The Greek word for Apostle.

Avarice: Excessive or insatiable desire for wealth, or gain. Also known as greed.

B

Benois Madonna: A painting started by Leonardo Da Vinci which depicts a super fat baby Jesus. Check it out.

Bizarrerie: Something of a bizarre quality. Made popular by the genius H.P. Lovecraft.

C

Castle Carcosa: Ficitonal city in the Ambrose Bierce short story, "An Inhabitant of Carcosa" (1891). Fun fact about Ambrose Bierce: he disappeared in Mexico and was never seen again. Creepy.

Castle Prospero: This is the Castle belonging to Prince Prospero from Edgar Allen Poe's short story entitled, "The Masque of the Red Death." The inhabitants of the castle lock themselves in to escape the black plague, only to find that the plague itself has already infiltrated the castle.

Cerberus: The famous three-headed Hell-hound that guards the gates of Hell. Also appears in *Harry Potter and the Sorcerer's Stone*, only this time under the name of Fluffy.

Communist Manifesto, The: The 1848 publication written by Karl Marx and Friedrich Engels. The perfect book for the comrade in your life.

D

Dank: Disagreeably damp, musty, and typically cold. Example: The inside of your ex-girlfriend's heart is dank.

Dr. Mengele: Josef Mengele, also known as "The Angel of Death," was a German doctor who determined who would be killed and who would be sent to forced labor in WWI. But what he is really famous for is performing human experiments on the camp inmates. Basically the slimiest of slime.

E

Eldritch: Weird or eerie. Example: Your grandmother giving me a kiss is eldritch.

F

Fraught: Laden with, or lousy with something.

Fonzie-esque: The ability to turn a jukebox on with a single fist pound.

G

Ghost Tree: Embodies Existentialism. The Ghost Tree is a manifestation of Existentialistic thought and ideas. The Ghost Tree is the sound of one hand clapping.

H

Hogarth: William Hogarth was an English painter, printer, satirist, and all around goofy guy. If somebody ever refers to your political cartoons as Hogarthian, you should take it as a compliment.

Holy Blood and the Holy Grail, The: A book by Michael Baigent, Richard Leigh, and Henry Lincoln. The book purports that the Holy Grail is actually a bloodline directly from Jesus and Mary Magdalene. See *The Da Vinci Code* for all of the "facts".

I

Immemorial: Extending or existing from beyond the reach of memory, record, or tradition. Something that is crazy old and crazy rare.

J

Jones, Mr.: Jim Jones, the famous cult leader of the Peoples Temple. Led his followers in a mass suicide resulting in 909 deaths, reminding us all not to drink the Kool-Aid.

Juggernaut: A literal or metaphorical force regarded as merciless or unstoppable. Or, an enemy of the X-Men.

K

Kilroy: An American pop-culture expression often seen in Graffiti. Popularized the phrase, "Kilroy was here."

Koimeterion: The sleeping place or cemetery.

L

Lackadaisical: Without interest, or determination. Also, a great word to use when you want to sound smart.

Lanirche: Lan-irshe. Another name for the Devil.

Lovelight: I wanted to juxtapose the name of the city with what the city really was like. It would be like me renaming the sewage waste department the potpourri palace. Brilliant.

Lurch: The faithful butler to the Addams family. A six foot, nine inch tall shambling gloomy butler who was more of a family member than a hired servant. He also stole the hearts of audience members everywhere.

M

Mein Kampf: Hitlers dumb book.

Mendacium: A lie, untruth, or fiction. What politicians tell us every day is Mendacium.

Metatron: Name of an Angel in Judaism and in some branches of Christian theology. Not to be confused with Megatron who is the leader of the Decepticons.

Monolithic: Formed of a single large block of stone. Very large and character-less.

Mors: In ancient Rome myth and literature, Mors is the personification of Death. Also, if you add an S and an E you get smores.

Mulciber: Roman god of blacksmithing. Rumored to have built the gates of Hell. He isn't real.

N

Noisome: Having an extremely offensive smell, or disagreeable and unpleasant. Example: The inside of Flava Flav's mouth is noisome.

O

Oscillating: To swing backward and forward like a pendulum.

Clamor: A loud and confused noise.

P

Padah: Hebrew for ransom, redeem, rescue, or deliver.

Pallid: Deficient in color, lacking sparkle of liveliness. Example: Conan O'Brien's face is pallid.

Pandemonium: A very noisy place. Also the capital of Hell in Paradise Lost. Avoid this place.

Paradise Lost: An epic poem by John Milton. It's an epic because it's crazy long. Read for your own edification.

Poem of the Man God: A book about 4,000 pages long on the life of Jesus Christ written by Maria Valtorta. She claimed to have visions in which the resurrected Christ visited her and dictated a book which she wrote down. At 4,000 pages though, you would think Jesus could have said it in fewer words.

Q

R

Rake's Progress, A: A series of eight paintings by William Hogarth. The paintings show the decline and fall of Tom Rakewell.

S

Shalom: The Hebrew word for peace. Give shalom a chance!

Similitude: An allegory or parable.

Skinless: A minion of Lanirche. Quite possibly Aleistar Crowley, or The Great Beast in life. In death, he is simply Lanirche's whipping boy.

Sychar: The town where Jesus meets the woman of Samaria in John 4:5-6.

T

Tenebrous: Shut off from the light, dark, or murky.

Tiriel: A character in the narrative poem by the same title written by William Blake.

U

Urantia Book, The: A spiritual and philosophical book written by various authors said to receive the message from divine beings. The book is 2,097 pages long. Go wikipedia that mess.

V

Vanity Fair: A town mentioned in John Bunyan's phenomenal book, *The Pilgrims Progress.* A city through which the King's Highway passes.

W

Wilde, Mr.: A repairer of reputations. A character in Robert W. Chambers book, *The King in Yellow.*

X

Y

Yellow King, The: A creature that personifies insanity, or the madness that comes with fame, fortune, progress, and knowledge. Borrowed from Robert W. Chambers. Please go read the book entitled *The King in Yellow,* if you enjoy great gothic literature.

Z

More Fiction
from Energion Publications

As a warning, for those who enjoy their stories to be nice, neat, and tidy with everything pulled together at the end, this book may frustrate you.
— **Alan Knox**, Blogger
    The Assembling of the Church

Is this humor? I stopped laughing twenty pages into this short little story. It hit too close to home ... Is there no escape from the Megabelt?
— **Lee Harmon**, Blogger
    The Dubious Disciple

It's easy to imagine "Covenant" as a family movie – with lots of angels in the air riding motorcycles and then later sliding down George Washington's nose at Mount Rushmore before appearing to comfort a little girl in a red hat.

The Message? The most important thing to do in your life is to form a relationship with God the Father and His Son, which brings with it the help of the heavenly host. It's a promise.
— **Rosemary K. Otzman**
    Belleville, Michigan *Independent*

More from Energion Publications

Personal Study

Evidence for the Bible	Elgin Hushbeck, Jr.	$16.99
Finding My Way in Christianity	Herold Weiss	$16.99
Holy Smoke, Unholy Fire	Bob McKibben	$14.99
Not Ashamed of the Gospel	Henry Neufeld	$12.99
The Jesus Paradigm	David Alan Black	$17.99
When People Speak for God	Henry Neufeld	$17.99

Christian Living

Directed Paths	Myrtle Neufeld	$7.99
Disciples: Jesus With Us	Riley Richardson	$7.99
Grief: Finding the Candle of Light	Jody Neufeld	$8.99
I Want to Pray!	Perry Dalton	$7.99
Soup Kitchen for the Soul	Renee Crosby	$12.99
The Sacred Journey	Chris Surber	$11.99
Will You Join the Cause of Global Missions?	David Alan Black	$4.99

Bible Study

Ephesians: A Participatory Study Guide	Bob Cornwall	$9.99
"In the Original Text It Says"	Ben Baxter	$9.99
Learning and Living Scripture	Geoffrey Lentz	$12.99
Philippians: A Participatory Study Guide	Bruce Epperly	$9.99
Luke: A Participatory Study Guide	Geoffrey Lentz	$8.99
Why Four Gospels?	David Alan Black	$11.99

Theology

Christian Archy	David Alan Black	$9.99
From Inspiration to Understanding	Edward W. H. Vick	$24.99
History and Christian Faith	Edward W. H. Vick	$9.99
Out of This World	Darren McClellan	$24.99
Ultimate Allegiance	Bob Cornwall	$9.99
The Questioning God	Ant Greenham	$9.99

Fiction

Covenant	Daniel Martin	$17.99
Megabelt	Nick May	$12.99
Prayer Trilogy	Kimberly Gordon	$9.99
Stories of the Way	Henry Neufeld	$9.99
Tales from Jevlir: Oddballs	Henry Neufeld	$7.99

Energion Publications — P.O. Box 841

Gonzalez, FL 32560

Website: http://energionpubs.com

Phone: (850) 525-3916

www.ingramcontent.com/pod-product-compliance
Lightning Source LLC
Chambersburg PA
CBHW051300250626
47155CB00009B/3377